The Reverend
Finds His Calling

by

Paula F. Winskye

This book is a work of fiction. Events and situations in this story are

purely fictional. Any resemblance to actual persons, living or dead

is coincidental.

"Leaving soon, Tony?"

Tony Wagner looked up from packing at the gray-haired man in the doorway of his dorm room.

"Yes, sir. I should be out of here in an hour or so."

"Your last summer of secular work."

"Yeah."

"Everyone has doubts about their career choice, Tony, be they doctors or truck drivers. We in the ministry may be more prone to doubts because of the responsibility that goes with the vocation."

"Yes, sir."

"Use this summer out in God's creation for prayerful consideration. The answer will come to you."

"Thanks. You always seem to know what to say."

"Years of practice. I was once a confused seminary student, just like you."

Tony smiled.

"Now, that's encouraging."

***

As Tony drove his decrepit Corolla from Wisconsin to Colorado, his thoughts turned back six years. Had it been that long? He still had vivid memories of that spring.

The torrent washed Tony off his feet, then gravity combined with the water, threatening to throw him into the flooding stream. Clawing at the slope, he found only mud. *God, please help me.* Just feet from the rising water, his right hand found an exposed tree root. He grabbed it with his left hand as well.

Working his way out of the muddy waterfall, his arms strained against the forces of nature. He reached a rock outcrop and sprawled on it, gasping. He had never been so exhausted in his nineteen years. He lay on the granite in the driving rain until he began shivering.

Tony forced himself to his feet. *I have to find shelter or I'll get hypothermia.* He studied the slope and chose a path littered with boulders and brush, anything but the slippery mud.

"Lord, thanks for the help. Don't stop now."

He tried to work his way back up the slope to get away from the flood, but the extra effort sapped his strength. Staying parallel to the stream would have to be good enough. He made frequent short rest stops.

The downpour continued. The gloom seemed closer to sunset than noon. Although he had hiked the area often, he knew very little about what shelter he might find in this valley. The hiking trails only crossed the creek four times.

Tony sank to a log, wondering how much farther he would have to go. *Could go.*

He sat up straighter. *What was that?* There again, faintly. A cry for help. He scrambled to his feet, exhaustion forgotten. Moving muffled the sound. But anyone in trouble had to be near the stream. He hurried as fast as conditions allowed.

"Help!" A female voice. "Someone please help me!"

Rounding a bend, he saw her clinging to a tree in the raging water. He groaned, but waved his arms.

"Over here!"

He saw hope in her muddy face. He sized up the situation while inching closer. The tree stood about thirty feet from shore. He could have easily pulled her out with a rope. Lacking that, he had no idea how to help her.

He shouted to be heard.

"Can you swim?"

"Not in this! I could walk out if I could stay on my feet."

"Hang on!" He looked around for a way to get her out and found no option but to go to her. "I'll be right there!"

"Okay! Hurry!"

He trudged upstream, trying to decide how far the current would carry him before he made it thirty feet from shore. *This should do it.* He waded into the boiling, brown water, grabbing a tree for stability. When it barely passed his knees, the current pulled him in. He swam desperately, but only succeeded in keeping his head above water. As he raced past, he heard her scream.

"No!"

At a bend in the creek, he reached for a tree leaning over the water. But the deluge slammed him against it harder than he had anticipated. He groaned, then forced himself to creep toward shore. In the shallows, he turned toward the girl and motioned for her to follow. She shook her head.

"I can't!"

Tony sighed and dragged himself back upstream, going farther this time. *I have to reach her on this try. I don't have the strength for another one.* This spot had three trees he could use to work his way out into the water.

The current caught him. This time he rushed toward her. But at the last second, the water swirled, threatening to wash him past again. He groped for something to stop him.

She seized his hand, slowing him just enough to let him grab the tree.

He inched closer to her.

"Hi."

"You're a sight for sore eyes."

"I'm always popular with a captive audience."

She laughed without humor.

"Now what?"

"After I rest a minute, we do the same thing I did before. The current carries us into that tree. We climb out of the water."

"I don't think I can."

"You have no choice. Just say a prayer and do it."

"Prayer?"

"You haven't been praying?"

"No."

"Well, start! We need all the help we can get." She nodded. "I'll go first so I can catch you when you come. The current will always carry you to the tree."

"Okay."

He waited a little longer, asking God to give him the strength to do this. As he prepared to take the wild ride again, she grabbed his shoulder. He turned and she kissed him quickly.

"Thanks, mister."

"Tony."

"Kelly."

He moved away from the tree and began swimming. Again, he hit hard. He planted his feet and, holding the tree with one hand, reached out to her with the other.

Still Kelly hesitated. She looked skyward and her lips moved before she left the tree. The torrent pulled her under, but she flailed her way to the surface. She kept her head above water until he caught her. She clung to him, coughing.

"Come on," he said.

They staggered to shore and collapsed in the mud.

***

Tony felt someone shaking him.

"Tony! We have to move. The water's still rising."

He nodded and struggled to his feet before helping her up. Walking did not make their shivers subside. Tony resolved to keep moving until they found shelter.

"Where are we going?"

"There should be a cabin along here somewhere."

"You don't know?"

"The hiking trails don't cross this valley much. But quite a few people have cabins in this area. There's bound to be some along the creek."

"I hope soon. I'm so cold."

"Me too. . . There!"

More of a house than a cabin, it sat well above the flood. Safe, but a steep climb. Renewed hope gave them strength. Tony noticed a stairway of timbers dug into the hillside, easing their way. They caught their breath under the deck before making the final climb. He tried the door, finding it locked as expected.

"Look for a key."

After trying the door mat, flower pot, and door frame, she found it under a concrete door stop. He stood at her shoulder while she tried to insert the key with shaking hand.

"You d-d-do it."

He took the key with an only slightly steadier hand. When he succeeded in opening the door, they spilled inside. He stripped off his shirt and t-shirt.

"Undress here. I'll find some towels."

"O-k-kay."

He kicked off his muddy shoes and peeled off wet jeans and socks. A search found a bathroom cabinet full of towels.

"Thank you, Lord." When he saw Kelly again, she had stripped completely. *That would probably shock me if I weren't so numb.* He handed her a towel. "I'll squeeze some of the water out of your hair before you start drying."

He removed the band from her pony tail along with some water, then put another towel around her shoulders, under her hair.

"Th-thanks."

"There's a clothes line on the deck. I'll hang our clothes there before I dry off. Maybe the rain will wash some of the mud out."

He hung the clothes, adding his underwear last. He closed the door and grabbed a towel. Kelly had moved closer to the fireplace, as if it were producing heat. He quickly dried himself and looked for matches. He found them on the mantle and paper for kindling next to a rack of split wood. As soon as the paper ignited, he opened the flue.

They pulled chairs as close as they could, soaking in every bit of warmth that the little flame produced. Quite a blaze developed before they moved back. When her teeth quit chattering, Kelly spoke.

"Thanks, Tony, for saving my life."

"Guess that's why God put me out here today."

"You must be a pretty religious guy."

"I try. But I'll admit that I'm more religious today than I was yesterday. This was pretty scary, even before I found you."

"Yeah. I was prepared for a little rain, not a monsoon."

"The forecast said a chance of *showers* today. You must not hike here very often. I'm here at least five days a week. I'd have seen you."

"I'm on my way home from college in Michigan. I'd seen the sign for this state park with hiking trails on other trips. Thought it'd be a nice break."

"I love this place. Usually. After a day of classes, I just want to get away from people."

"I didn't see another car in the lot."

"The park borders campus. A trail starts a hundred yards from my dorm. At least your car's high and dry in that lot."

"And I suppose the park rangers will notice it and look for me when they can."

"Whenever that is. But we're safe and drying. If we're lucky, the owners left some food here."

"I suppose they shut off the water for the winter."

"They may have turned it on again. There's no dust."

"What does dust have to do with water?"

"They've been here cleaning. Maybe they turned on the water too."

He walked to the kitchen sink and found water. Then he flipped a light switch. No electricity.

"I suppose the storm knocked it out," she said. "Will anyone miss you?"

He began opening cupboard doors.

"My dorm mates. Some of them saw me leave. When I'm not back by dark, they'll report it. Want a candy bar?"

"I'd kill for one."

He grinned and brought it to her.

"Don't say that. I might think I'm trapped with a homicidal maniac."

"Only if you don't give me one of those candy bars."

He laughed and they devoured the chocolate.

"I'll see if they left us any clothes."

"I'll just stay here."

He found a terry cloth robe in the bathroom and brought it to her.

"You can have this. I'll keep looking."

"Bless you."

In the first bedroom he discovered an extra large flannel shirt on a hook. He pulled it on and rolled up the sleeves before searching the dresser. He combed the second bedroom and found the third converted to an office.

"They don't leave a lot of clothes here during the winter. Slipper socks for you and socks for me."

"Works for me. That shirt's long enough, you wouldn't need a towel."

"May get a little drafty. I'll dry some of these towels by the fire. A dry one would feel good."

"Will the stove work?"

"If the gas is on. We should just have to light it manually. If not, we'll have to cook in the fireplace."

"Is there anything to cook?"

"So far I found rice. But I didn't get through all the cupboards."

"I'll pry myself away from the fire." She searched while he hung towels. "Tuna, tuna dinner in a box, mac and cheese, dried fruit, spices, hot cocoa, and tea. We won't starve. Would you see if you can start a burner for me? I'm leery of gas stoves."

"Okay. Mind if I ask you some questions?"

"Sure."

"What's your major?"

"Natural resources. I want to work in a national park."

"I've considered that major. I'll be working in a national park out west this summer."

"I'm jealous. How'd you land that job?"

"I know someone."

"So what's your major?"

"Aerospace."

"Your taking up space until you decide what you want to do?"

"Yeah."

"What other majors are you considering?"

"Law enforcement or theology."

"You want to be a priest?"

"Minister."

"So you don't have to give up sex?"

He smiled.

"They just prefer I get married first."

"Oh. I'll make tuna hot dish for supper. Where you from?"

"About thirty miles down the road."

"I'm from Fargo, North Dakota. No jokes, please."

"Wouldn't dream of it."

***

Tony dragged a mattress to the fireplace. The owners had also left them plenty of blankets and pillows. He and Kelly surrendered to exhaustion and turned in early. He thought that snuggling with her might prove too stimulating, but sleep came quickly.

Tony opened his eyes. *I was right.* Even in his sleep, her presence had effected his body. *If she wakes now, she'll think I plan to rape her.*

I'd better get out of here.

As he pulled away, she rolled on her back.

"Where you going?"

"Um-m. I . . . I . . . I'm sorry."

"I can help you with that."

She untied her robe and let it fall open. He groaned.

"I don't want to."

"I'm not forcing you. I just wanted to let you know you have options. You don't have to suffer."

He froze except for his heaving chest. *Who am I kidding? I want to.* He nearly leaped on her, completely failing to hide his inexperience. It ended almost before it began.

"I'm sorry. I'm not very good at that."

"You haven't done it very much, have you."

"I can't count the number of times on one hand anymore."

"I thought it might be your first."

The dim light hid his blush.

"I'm sorry."

"Quit apologizing." She touched his lips. "This time will be for me. I'll teach you how to please a woman."

"But, can I do it again so soon?"

"A guy your age can do it all day and night."

"I can?"

"Uh-huh. Are you ready to learn?"

"I shouldn't."

"Okay. But you owe me some foreplay. Just touch me gently. When you find a spot I like, keep working on it."

"How will I know if you like it?"

"Oh, you'll know."

He experimented, finding her response to his touch fascinating.

"You're not just faking this, are you?"

"Oh, no. You have a gentle touch. You just needed guidance."

He continued and soon reacted to her response. She looked pleased.

"You *knew* this would happen."

"No. But given a willing, naked woman, I figured there was a ninety-nine percent chance that it would." She sat up and began unbuttoning his shirt. "This time I want to see that hard body."

"I shouldn't."

She pushed his shirt off.

"Nice. It's your choice. But you'll be amazed how much better it'll be this time."

She lay back. For nearly a minute, he stared at her. *I have to see if she's right.*

***

Tony woke and listened to the rain. *I think it's slowed.* He replaced his shirt and added wood to the fire. He watched Kelly sleep before tucking the blankets around her. He walked to the window and stared at the steady drizzle, which darkened the sky even at nine a.m. The creek had risen more during the night. A log jam of uprooted trees lay just downstream.

It'd probably be a good idea to check the foundation, just to be safe. He undressed completely and ventured into the rain. At the bottom of the stairs, he observed little gullies along the foundation, no threat to the building's underpinning. He climbed back to the deck and stopped to squeeze water from their clothes before going inside.

"Interesting choice of rain gear," Kelly said.

"Easy to dry."

"Looks good too."

Tony grabbed a towel from the fireplace.

"We're in no danger of sliding down the hill."

"Reassuring."

"I'll put some water on for breakfast."

"Hot chocolate sounds good."

"Yeah."

"I found toothpaste last night. Guess I'll use my finger to brush my teeth."

When Kelly returned from the bathroom, she lugged a five gallon pail of water.

"Need help with that?"

"No. I'm fine." She placed it near the fire, then held her hand against the fire side of the pail. "I want warm water, but I don't want to melt the bucket."

"We could heat some on the stove."

"I'll probably do that too. I want to wash my hair later."

"Great idea."

"How long you think it'll be before we can get out of here?"

"Maybe twenty-four hours after the rain stops. We'll have to cross the creek to get to your car, so we have to wait for it to go down."

"I think the rain's almost stopped now."

"Hey, it has!"

"Is my car closer than your campus?"

"Yeah. It's maybe a mile to your car, more than three miles to town."

"What's your favorite color?"

"Green. Why?"

"Thought we'd get to know each other better. Mine's blue, like your eyes."

"Sounds like a sex starter to me."

"If I want sex, I don't need to talk. Are you a farm boy or a city kid?"

"Farmer."

"Dairy farm?"

"No, believe it or not. We raise apples, melons, sweet corn, and pumpkins. And we sell hay to dairy farmers."

"That's cool. My dad's a welder. He builds four-wheel drive tractors. Mom's an accountant. What's your last name?"

"Wagner."

She opened the cupboard to retrieve mugs and hot cocoa mix.

"Mine's Holiday."

"Not a real common name."

"Yeah. Good thing my parents didn't name me Mary or something silly like that. You look like a jock."

"I played basketball during the winter. The rest of the year, my sports involve horses. My mom's really into endurance riding. You have to be in good shape for that."

"I know. I like horses too. I usually showed in timed events because I didn't have to worry about the judge playing favorites."

"Amazing. We have something in common. Can't learn that when you're making out."

"You have a sarcastic sense of humor." She brought cocoa and dried fruit to the table. "I suppose you're a Packer fan."

He pretended to take off a hat and place it over his heart.

"I have a poster of Brett Favre on my bedroom wall. We always go to church on Sunday, but if the Packers play at noon, dinner is frozen pizza.

Mom isn't going to miss the game."

"She sounds like a great mom. There are plenty of Packer fans where I'm from. But most of us root for the Vikings. My mom could care less. She usually goes shopping Sunday afternoon. She finally quit asking me to go along."

"I'll forgive you for rooting for the enemy. Football's the second thing we have in common."

"Are you a freshman?"

"Yeah."

"That's three. And we're both interested in the environment. We have a lot in common."

"The rain's stopped. I'll squeeze the water out of our clothes and bring them by the fireplace to dry."

"Sounds like a plan. This afternoon, I'll boil water in all the kettles and we can take a bath."

***

After mixing cold and boiling water in the over-sized tub, Kelly put more on the stove, then sent Tony for the bucket while she washed her hair.

"Okay. Rinse me off." He poured water over her long, brown hair. "Oh! That's cold!"

"I'll get the rest of the hot water."

When he returned, she motioned for him to join her.

"I'll wash your hair."

"I can wash my own hair."

"I know. This will be more fun."

"Whatever."

After he soaked his blond hair, she kneeled behind him to perform the task.

"Now, doesn't that feel good?"

"Yeah. I'll try to scrub the mud off my feet. Wonder if I'll ever get clean." He kept his back to her. When she began washing his back, his spine stiffened. "You don't have to do that."

"You can do mine when we're finished."

She slid her lathered hands around his waist and blew in his ear. More than his spine stiffened. He did not protest this time. *She'll ignore me and I'll let my body take over, so why bother?*

***

They left the cold bathroom to dry off by the fire. Tony sighed.

"Must be deer season."

"Deer season?"

"You're the hunter and I'm the buck in rutt. You use the right lure and I disengage my brain and engage my sex drive."

She laughed.

"Don't feel bad. That's typical of guys your age. You actually think a little more than most of them."

"Right!"

"No, really. You *noticed* that I'm pushing your buttons and you actually *care*. The rest of them would only care that they were getting all they could handle."

He pulled on his shirt.

"Oh. Guess you have a lot of experience."

"With one guy. But I've watched the rest. The word 'no' isn't in their vocabulary. I know if I hadn't been willing, you wouldn't have tried to change my mind."

"Not me. But I should have at least thought about protection."

"I guess you have. Do you give blood?"

"Blood? Yeah?"

"Me too. Have you been with anyone since the last time you gave blood?"

He frowned.

"No."

"Same here. Has your blood ever been rejected?"

"Not that I know of."

"They'd tell you if it was. I've never been rejected either, so we're not going to catch anything from each other."

"Oh. That's a relief. Still. It's pretty stupid to have unprotected sex with a stranger."

"Stupid for both of us. You're not the only one who disengaged your brain."

"So, can we stop this now?"

"Why? Just enjoy yourself for another day. Then I'll be out of your life forever. You're having fun, aren't you."

Tony gazed at the fire.

"I've never felt so good. And so bad at the same time."

She wrapped her arms around him under his shirt.

"Keep thinking about that good feeling."

***

The next morning, with the sun warming them, they hiked along the ridge, having left a note and money for the cabin owner. They had an easy trip until they needed to cross the valley and creek. They slid down the muddy slope. An uprooted tree provided a bridge across the still-swollen creek.

Climbing the far slope presented the biggest challenge. They rested three times before reaching the top, then rested again. Two hundred yards more and they reached the parking lot.

Kelly pulled her keys from her pocket.

"I can't believe you didn't lose those in the flood."

"Tight jeans. Would you play lookout while I change clothes?"

"Yeah. You have plenty in there."

"If I can find what I need in that mess. Can I give you a ride back to town?"

"No. You're headed the other direction. If no one picks me up, it'll feel good to walk on pavement."

"I hear you. But you saved my life. The least I could do is give you a ride."

"You gave me plenty."

She smiled and pulled on a t-shirt.

"I suppose so. Have a nice life, Tony."

"You too. Take a few more precautions with men."

"Good advice."

She gave him a long kiss before driving away.

***

Tony stopped the Corolla in the driveway beside towering spruce trees. The ranch style house shared an acre lot with so many trees that he could not see the houses on either side or across the street. Dense forest abutted the backyard.

He unfolded his six foot, two inch frame and stretched.

"Tony! How's our favorite tenant?"

Tony smiled at Gil Simon, a rugged, always red-faced man in his fifties.

"I'm tired."

"It's always a long drive."

"Tony!" Gil's petite wife, Betty, scurried out the front door to give him a hug. "We've missed you."

"I've missed you too, Betty. I've missed everything about Spruce Lake."

"What's not to miss? The only thing I regret about moving here eight years ago is that we didn't do it sooner. Gil, help Tony with his stuff. I'll set another place for supper."

"Yes, ma'am."

"Did you have many boarders this winter?" Tony asked.

"Our fair share. Twenty-seven, I believe. One pair stayed two weeks. They liked being able to ski right out the front door."

"That's a good winter for you. Did you do more advertising?"

"In a couple of cross-country ski magazines. Best investment we could of made. How's the Bible study going?"

"The usual. I'm still not sure if it's my calling. I need to decide by the end of the summer."

"You got a deadline now?"

"Self-imposed. It wouldn't be fair of me to graduate, then decide not to be a minister."

"I'd expect that kind of thoughtfulness from you."

"This is the last of it."

"Good. Now we can sit down to some lemonade while Betty finishes supper."

"How's everything here?"

"Same old same old. Don's ornery as ever. Ryan got elected again last fall. Kevin and Jean had twins last month."

"Twins! Again!"

"Beats all, doesn't it. Four kids in three years. They swear they're done now."

"I guess."

Gil poured lemonade and they sat by the table. Betty offered further news.

"Norris got a job in Yellowstone. His replacement's supposed to start soon."

"Anybody I know?"

"No. Don said he came from Roosevelt Park in North Dakota."

"Oh. I'll meet him soon enough. I'm beat. I won't unpack any more than I have to. Don't want to oversleep on my first day back."

"You keep coming for supper until you get settled."

"Thanks, Betty. I promise it won't be more than a week."

"Won't bother us if it is."

***

The next morning Tony walked eight blocks, the width of the town, to park headquarters. Located five miles inside the boundary of Evergreen National Park, Spruce Lake pre-dated the park by forty years. The town's entire economy depended on the park and tourism. During the summer the population swelled with seasonal employees.

Since real estate rarely became available and brought top dollar, nearly every home owner had added an apartment or sleeping room. No one wanted to construct apartment buildings to sit empty eight months of the year.

At 7:30, Tony walked up the steps of the log ranger station and directly to the coffee pot to fill his mug.

"Morning, reverend!"

Tony grinned, but changed it to a scowl before joining Don Storm in his office. With gray hair and beard, his boss could have retired years ago.

But he had dedicated his life to the park, tagging along with the rangers since his tenth birthday, joining the staff as a summer worker at sixteen.

"Morning, you old reprobate. Haven't they kicked you out of here yet?"

"They'll have to carry me out feet first. If they try to get rid of me while I'm still breathing, I'll sue 'em for age discrimination."

"You probably would. What's new?"

"We got a new full-time girl starting tomorrow. I'll have you show her the ropes."

"Why not one of the full-time guys?"

"Because you won't hit on her. We don't want to scare her off the first day."

"Kevin wouldn't hit on her."

"He's taking tomorrow off to help Jean take the new twins for a check-up. You hear about that?"

"Of course. Betty filled me in."

"Here's something she didn't tell you about." Don pulled a paper from his desk. "You hear about a murder up in Glacier last fall?"

"I think I heard something about it."

"Well, over the past couple years there was one in Yosemite and another in Cascade, same M.O."

"A serial killer?"

"They're leaning that way. The victims were robbed. Whoever killed them is a sick bastard. They were all shot four or five times before they died."

"Hope he stays away from here."

"That's exactly why I'm telling you. They've sent this alert to all the parks. We're supposed to report any missing persons to the FBI right away."

"Kind of over-reacting, aren't they?"

"What can I say, it's the government. You and Jeff can bring the horses in this afternoon. He's been riding them for a couple weeks, so there should be no surprises."

"Any changes there?"

"We sold Diamond before he hurt somebody."

"Good."

"His replacement's just five, but he seems level-headed."

"Anybody got the stalls ready?"

"Not yet."

"I'll do it as soon as I finish my coffee."

"Good man."

When Tony left the building he heard an unmistakable rumble, blocks away. As he crossed the yard it grew louder. He wondered about the identity of the Harley rider. Only one lived here, but they saw tourist bikers every summer. When the bike turned into park headquarters, he recognized the blond mustache, leather vest, and forearm tatoo. Tony grinned as he shut off his engine.

"You'll never sneak up on anybody riding that."

"You don't ride a hog to sneak. You ride to be seen and heard."

"How'd you ever get elected sheriff?"

Ryan laughed and removed his helmet.

"My credentials outweighed looking like a gang member. Course, going to church every Sunday, joining the PTA, and volunteering for every fund raiser in town helped. How you been?"

"Surviving. Heard you won another election."

"The first one's hardest. After that, if you don't screw up too bad, it's a piece of cake."

"Anything exciting happening in law enforcement around here."

"Never. I'd better let you get back to work. Thought I'd stop and say 'hi' while I took my first ride this spring."

"Aren't you a little underdressed for this time of year?"

"I'm just cruising around town. I'll put my leathers on before I hit the road this afternoon. Later."

***

The next day, Tony fed the horses before entering the ranger station for coffee. Don shouted his usual greeting.

"Don, can't you use my name?"

From his angle, Tony saw the back of a woman with short, brown hair, seated in Don's office.

"Oh, don't be such a grouch, reverend. Come in here and meet Kelly."

The name made his heart skip a beat. He grinned at the silliness of his reaction. Then she faced him and he froze, slack-jawed.

"Hi," Kelly said.

"Tony Wagner, meet Kelly Thiel." She smiled while Tony continued to stare. "Well, I didn't think a pretty girl could leave the reverend tongue-tied. Oh, I'm being politically incorrect. A pretty female ranger."

Kelly grinned.

"Just don't call me an ugly girl. But my looks aren't Tony's problem. We've met."

"Really? I'd like to hear about that."

Tony snapped out of his trance.

"Long time ago. Hi, Kelly. Welcome to Evergreen. A little different from Roosevelt."

"Big difference. More like Michigan and Wisconsin."

"This country's more interesting than Wisconsin. Wait till you see some of the views."

"Give her the driving tour this afternoon, when you check the campgrounds."

"Okay. Ready for the headquarters tour, Kelly?"

"Let the girl finish her coffee."

"She can walk and drink coffee at the same time."

"He's always like this, Kelly. Can't just sit around and collect a check like the rest of us government employees."

Kelly laughed.

"I'll see you later, Don."

She refilled her cup before following Tony outside. He asked the first question that came to mind.

"Have you married since . . . ?"

"No-o. I may not have been cautious about who I slept with, but I was careful about giving out my real name."

"Oh. I suspected that. A couple years later, I tried to find you."

"You did?"

"It weighed on my conscience. My advisor suggested that I find you to help put it behind me. I searched graduating classes from all the Fargo schools, even West Fargo. I looked at pictures in case you'd given me a false name."

"You needed to go ten miles more. Mapleton."

"Oh."

"Your name tag says, M. Wagner. What's with that?"

"Milton. When I was nine, I decided it wasn't cool enough. I wanted to be called Tony. Even my parents went along. They drew the line when I wanted to legally change it at sixteen. They said they'd support me if I did it as an adult. I decided it wasn't that important."

"I would never have thought of Tony as short for Milton."

They had reached the stable.

"These are the horses."

"That's good to know."

"I'm sorry. You really threw me for a loop."

"Would it help if I apologized? I seduced you. Back then, I liked having that power over guys. I was pretty immature."

"Thanks. Maybe it does help. I'll get past this. I'd accepted that I'd never see you again. It'll take me a while to adjust. You didn't seem shocked to see me."

"I was prepared. Don said your name before you came in. I remembered you had a job in a park out west."

Tony made a face.

"O-kay. This is useless. I can't seem to think of a thing to tell you. Try asking me questions."

She smiled.

"I'll do that for you."

***

Tony felt in a fog the rest of the day. He even let Kelly drive when they serviced the campgrounds, afraid that he would put the truck through a guard rail.

After work, he walked the perimeter streets, covering two miles before reaching his apartment. It did nothing to clear his head. He said an absent-minded "hello" to Betty before descending the stairs.

"Why am I acting like an idiot?"

You're afraid people will find out you're not the perfect seminary student they think you are. He had to admit the truth of that. Everyone here knew him as the church-going young man who helped elderly ladies with their chores and filled in when the pastor went on vacation. They had never even seen him date. News of a wild sexual weekend would probably make them faint.

He had wanted to find Kelly and deal with that part of his past. *But I didn't want to have to deal with it every day. God doesn't always answer prayers the way we'd like him to.*

He decided a cool shower might snap him out of his mood. But nothing seemed to help. He tapped his forehead against the wall several times and turned off the water. He had to talk to someone about this. He wrapped himself in a towel and dialed a number.

"Parsonage," the gravelly voice said.

"Hi, Pastor Johnson. It's Tony."

"Hello, Tony. I heard you were back."

"A couple days. I work the next two weekends, then I'm available every third Sunday if you need an usher."

"Wonderful. I plan to be gone July 14th. Will Don give you the day off to take the service for me?"

"Yeah. But maybe you'll change your mind after I tell you something."

"Is there a problem?"

"I guess my past has caught up with me."

"Would you like to come over now?"

"That'd be great. I can be there in about fifteen minutes."

"Good. Plan to stay for supper."

"Thanks."

***

Tony changed to jeans and a Packers sweatshirt, told Betty his destination, and walked four blocks to the parsonage. Even after being side-tracked three times by residents welcoming him back, in fifteen minutes he sat in the pastor's study recounting his history with Kelly. Pastor Johnson listened without comment until he finished.

"We all have things in our past we aren't proud of. Although I'll admit that mine isn't quite as colorful as yours."

Tony smiled.

"I always put pastors on pedestals."

"We all have feet of clay. My father thought I was destined for jail rather than the pulpit. So you see, you're not alone in your youthful indiscretions. The Lord forgives you. You need to forgive yourself."

"Thanks. But what will other people think?"

"Will Kelly tell them?"

"I don't think so. She's not proud of it either."

"Then I see no reason for you to share it. By telling me, you've lifted the burden of the secret you carried. It happened before you came here. You don't need to apologize for it."

"Thanks."

"Tony, when was your last date?"

Tony squirmed.

"Date? Why?"

"Because it may relate to why this has left you so flustered."

"My first year of seminary. The next day I got a D on my Hebrew test. I've really had to work hard to get good grades. I don't have time to date."

"You have time now."

"I guess so. But I thought I'd just wait until I graduate."

"How many of your classmates are married?"

Tony shrugged.

"About half."

"How many of the rest are engaged or have a steady girlfriend?"

"Most of them."

"God did not intend for man to be alone. A God-fearing woman smooths over the bumps in life. She shares your burdens. The benefits of a relationship far outweigh the complications."

Tony studied the floor.

"Dating scares me."

The pastor chuckled.

"Understandable. This Wednesday is the monthly potluck. There are four eligible young ladies in the church. Strike up conversations with them instead of the women old enough to be your grandmother."

"I could do that."

"You're a very charming young man. Focus that charm where it can benefit you."

"I'm just afraid it'll benefit me too much."

"I see. Then church is a safe place to experiment."

"Yeah. I'll give it a try."

***

"Tony! Get in here!"

Tony knew exactly what had Don up in arms. He hurried to Don's office.

"Yes, sir."

As planned, his uncommon response deflected some of Don's anger.

"Don't try to distract me. What the hell's wrong with you? You've been wandering around in a daze since last week. Since Thursday when Kelly got here. You got the hots for her?"

"No. I'm sorry. I think I'm getting better. I'm sorry."

"Close the door. Sit down. Spill it."

Tony settled into a chair. He took a deep breath, then another, before words came.

"You remember my story about the flood?"

"Who could forget that?" Don's jaw dropped. "Kelly's the girl who lit you up?"

"Yeah."

Don laughed, then turned serious.

"You can't believe this is a coincidence."

Tony shrugged.

"This was her major and what she wanted to do. On the other hand, my faith doesn't allow for coincidences. God knew I needed closure on that episode of my life. But all I'm getting are a bunch of really wild memories."

"Well, reverend, you're just full of surprises. You do qualify for inclusion in the male gender. So what do you plan to do to get your brains out of your pants?"

Tony blushed.

"Pastor Johnson says I should start dating. I guess to take my mind off Kelly."

"Not a bad approach. Tina down at the Elkhorn is a hot little number."

"I don't think that's exactly what he had in mind. There's some single women in church."

"Most of them are collecting Social Security."

"There's young ones too. Liza."

"She's pretty."

"Jan and Anna."

"Schoolmarms. Kind of tame."

"And, what's her name, Felicity?"

"Felicia. She's a smart gal. You could have any of 'em on her back in no time."

"Don! That's not the goal."

"Sure, it is. That's every man's goal. You'll just probably take a more round about way to get there. Marriage, and all that."

"Like you did."

"I was young and stupid."

"That's why you've been married forty years."

"Now I'm old and stupid. I don't care how you do it. I just want to see my dependable reverend by next Monday."

"I should be able to deliver."

"Now, get to work." Tony left and Don rifled through a file cabinet, pulling out a folder. He studied it with a grin. "Reverend, you're in for the shock of your life."

***

Wednesday evening, Tony brought the same dish he always brought to the potluck, a fruit salad using canned fruit and a box of gelatin. He received hugs from a half-dozen silver-haired ladies, then sought out those closer to his age. To his surprise, all four were present. *Guess they don't have a social life either.*

When he struck up conversations with Jan and Liza, they became tongue-tied. Jan recovered quickly, but Liza managed only one word answers. Anna and Felicia reacted better, but he saw that he surprised both by talking to them. They had no shortage of things to discuss. Jan and Anna had attended the same college where he was a student. Everyone liked to talk about the park.

He followed them through the food line and managed to sit near three of the four. Their smiles and an occasional blush told him that his charm worked just fine. When they finished eating, he helped clear tables. One of his favorite "grandmothers" poked him with an elbow.

"Tony's courting."

He blushed.

"Just be quiet, Clarice. The pastor told me I needed to spend time with ladies my own age."

"That's called courting. Good for you. They've been waiting for you to notice them."

"They have?"

"Look in the mirror. They're already eating out of your hand."

His face turned a little redder.

"Has everybody noticed?"

"Don't know if they all have. All of us old hags have. You usually flirt with us."

"Sorry."

"Oh, we're happy to see it. We've been wondering when you'd wake up and smell the perfume."

"Is everybody that concerned about my social life?"

"Just us old biddies. Hasn't your mama wondered why you don't have a girlfriend?"

"She asks every time I talk to her."

"There you go. Good looking man like yourself should have a wife. And if he doesn't, he should have them following him around like puppies."

"So why haven't you said anything before?"

"Twern't none of my business."

"But it is now?"

"Just trying to encourage you."

"Thanks, Clarice."

***

"You seem a little more relaxed," Kelly said.

Tony grinned.

"I'm getting used to you."

"Let me guess. You don't take this long to get used to everyone."

"No."

"I haven't tried to jump your bones."

He blushed.

"Yeah."

"I really have changed. I'm not that girl anymore."

"I believe you. I'm sorry I acted so spacy there for a while."

"We're okay now?"

"Yeah."

"Good. Because I think we can be friends. You're an awful nice guy, Tony."

"Thanks. Let's take a ride this afternoon. You need to learn the trails and it's quicker on horseback."

"Great. Riding is my favorite part of being a ranger."

"Mine too."

"Do you still do endurance riding?"

"Don't have time. Seminary keeps me pretty busy."

"That must be a long course of study. I thought you'd have graduated by now."

"I didn't make up my mind for another year. After I worked here that first summer, I transferred to Vermilion Community College in Ely, Minnesota. I took Peace Officer Training with NPS courses. I spent the next three summers here as a Seasonal Law Enforcement ranger."

"But you're not carrying a gun now."

"No. Don asked me to go back to interpretive work."

"So when do you graduate from the seminary?"

"I have one more year of classes, then I spend a year as a vicar. If I decide to finish."

"You still haven't made up your mind?"

"No. I still like being out here better than being with a bunch of people."

"You must have enough experience to get a full-time Park Service job."

"I don't think I want to go to another park. I like this place. I like the people. Maybe I'll apply if a position opens up."

"I'd like to see you stay."

He studied her.

"Why?"

"I like you. Now that we've found each other again, I don't want to lose a friend."

***

They returned from their ride with just enough time to care for their horses before the end of their work day. Kelly smiled at him.

"You were right about the beautiful country. Today made me really happy that I took this job. Eventually, I want to get my own horse so I can ride on my days off."

"We can ride these on our days off. Don has a one person, one horse policy. That way if a horse starts having problems, he knows who to blame. That means nobody will be riding your horse when you're not working."

"Great. Would you like to come to my place for something cold to drink?"

Tony shifted from one foot to the other.

"No, thank you."

"Are you still afraid of me?"

"No. As a seminary student, I'm held to higher standards. I can't just spend time at a woman's house alone."

"Oh. I see. It's not just me. They don't want you thumping headboards with anyone."

Tony blushed.

"No. Want to stop by the Dairy Queen instead?"

"I'll take a rain check. I'll put some chairs on my front lawn so next time I invite you, we can stay in the public eye."

"That sounds like a plan."

"I'll see you tomorrow."

***

Tony finished repairing the trail marker and headed downhill toward the parking lot, meeting a hiker carrying a huge pack.

"Morning, sir. Are you planning to camp in the back country?"

"Hell, no. I didn't hike this far to be eaten by a bear. I'll stick to the patrolled campgrounds."

Tony smiled.

"I understand. You filled out a registration form?"

"Of course."

"Well, enjoy your hike."

When he reached the parking lot, he saw a massive, luxury SUV. All the latest high-end hiking equipment. Tony recognized money when the back packer gestured to him.

"Can I help you, sir?"

"Yeah. I see on this map that there are two trails leading to Eagle's Roost. Which do you recommend?"

"That depends on what you're looking for, sir. Most people take Lava Flow Trail. It's enough of a challenge for the average hiker. Sky Line Trail is much more rugged, more climbing, some cliff-hugging stretches. We recommend that no one hike it alone. But the views are breath-taking."

"Sky Line Trail it is, then. Thanks."

"You're welcome, sir. Don't forget to fill out a registration form, so we know where you're going and when you expect to return."

"I don't report my coming and going to anyone."

"Well, sir, if you're planning to be gone two weeks, we don't want to start searching for you on Monday."

"Oh, good point."

"Thank you, sir."

"Will my Navigator be safe in this lot?"

"It's lighted and there are two security cameras."

"Good enough."

"Have a safe trip, sir."

***

"Good morning, ladies," Tony said, standing at the main entrance to the church in a shirt and tie.

Anna and Liza smiled at him, flirting. He had managed to go for walks with both Liza and Jan and help Anna till her garden. No real dates, but progress. They entered the church and he greeted other parishioners.

"Tony," Pastor Larson motioned to him. "We may have guests with tourist season here. Would you get the extra hymnals from the school?"

"Yes, sir."

Tony returned as the organist began to play. He and the other usher stayed in the entryway, waiting for stragglers, until the congregation had nearly finished singing the first hymn. From his vantage point in the back of the church, he had become very good at identifying people by the backs of their heads. He recognized most, and tried to identify the rest during the hymns.

The back of one female head looked familiar, but not in this setting. He did not recognize Kelly until he saw her face while passing the offering plate. Once again she left him off balance. He could not imagine, given what he knew of her, that she had been raised in a church of this conservative denomination.

Of course, Spruce Lake offered only two choices. Many visitors came here simply because they were not Catholic. To attend a church of any other denomination involved a thirty mile drive. Today he saw nearly a dozen non-member residents. Satisfied with that explanation, he relaxed and thought little of her until he walked forward to dismiss the parishioners.

As he worked his way back, Tony realized that the little blond boy beside Kelly was *with* Kelly. *How old is he?* The other usher elbowed him and Tony nodded to dismiss the next pew. The boy had to be about five. *Five!* Tony nodded to the next row, leaving a good view of the boy's face. He looked just like his father. *Oh, God!*

Kelly smiled. Not a gloating smile. Nothing spiteful about it. An understanding smile with an apology in her eyes. He took a deep breath, relieved that he only had two more pews to dismiss. When he finished, he asked the other usher to do the few little chores that followed the service.

He stood at the top of the steps searching for Kelly.

He spotted her with her son--his son--in the school yard across the street. The walk seemed endless. She encouraged him with another smile. Tony's voice cracked.

"Is this why you wanted me to come to your place?"

"Yeah. Brett, this is my friend Tony."

"Hi, Tony."

"Hi, Brett. That's a pretty neat name."

"Mommy named me after Brett Favre because my daddy is a Packer fan."

Tony swallowed.

"I'm a big Packer fan too."

"I like football."

"Tony, would you like to have lunch with us?"

"Yes."

"You're not worried about what people will think?"

"I don't care."

"Brett, let's go home." He ran ahead of his parents, who walked in silence for a block. Kelly tried to explain. "I wasn't sure if I had the nerve to come into church. Then I saw you go across the street. I didn't know you'd be ushering. I'm sorry about that."

"You came here because of me, didn't you."

"I saw your picture in the National Park magazine. It said you were a summer employee. I hoped you'd be back for another summer. I figured even if you weren't, I'd be able to get to know you better through your friends, and eventually find you."

"How long have you been looking for me?"

"I wasn't. I quit looking when Brett was about a year old. That's when I quit feeling sorry for myself. That Milton threw me off. I looked for Anthony and Antonio. Never thought of Milton. I just stumbled on you in the magazine."

"Oh. He's my son."

"No doubt about that."

"I want to be his father."

"Good."

"I don't make much, but I'll help as much as I can."

"I know. I know you'll be a good father. I'm sorry this will ruin your reputation."

"I don't care. Nothing's more important than Brett. It's unreal. He's already grabbed my heart."

"I see that. I shouldn't be surprised."

"Will you tell him I'm his father?"

"After a while. When I told him we were moving, I promised him he'd get to meet his daddy before long. Glad you didn't make me a liar. Here we are. Brett, why don't you show Tony your toys while I get lunch on the table."

"Okay. Come on, Tony."

Tony sat on the floor and played with Brett. He listened intently to his son's narrative, trying to make up for lost time. He resisted the urge to hug Brett, not wanting to confuse him. While they ate their sandwich lunch, he could not take his eyes off his son. Brett smiled.

"Are you a ranger too, Tony?"

"Yeah. For now. I haven't decided what I want to be when I grow up."

Brett giggled.

"You are growed up."

"Do you think so?"

"Yeah. You're big."

"What do you want to be when you grow up?"

"A ranger. Or a football player. I like horses."

"Me too."

"Mommy says we're going to your church now. We didn't go that much before."

"Church is good for us. We learn things we need to know."

"Do you go every Sunday?"

"When I don't have to work."

"Mommy works some too. I go to day care across the street. This year I start kindergarten."

"Wow. You're a big boy already."

"Uh-huh. Mommy, can I be done now?"

"You ate very good. Go wash your hands, then you can play in the back yard."

Tony waited until he left the room.

"Is he okay? I mean, healthy and everything."

"Just fine. The usual childhood stuff. His pre-school screenings were normal for his age. That's a relief."

"Yeah. Is he always so well-behaved?"

"Oh, he has his moments. But I think he's a pretty good kid, thanks to my parents. I transferred to NDSU and lived with them after I found out I was pregnant." She interrupted the story when Brett returned and they walked to the back yard. "They agreed to take care of him if I was attending classes or working. I had to hire a babysitter if I wanted a social life. They called it the consequences of my actions. I resented that until his first birthday. Then I grew up."

"Tony, push me!" Brett called from the swing. Tony pushed Brett as long as he wanted. They both rejoined Kelly. "Mommy, I'm thirsty."

"I'll get us some juice. You stay here with Tony."

"Okay."

Brett's eyes nearly bored through Tony.

"What do you see?"

"Is Tony short for something?"

"Milton."

"Oh."

"Why?"

"My middle name's Anthony. Sometimes people say Tony."

"That's usually what Tony's short for. I just wanted to be different."

"Oh. Are you my daddy?"

Tony looked toward the door. No Kelly.

"What makes you say that?"

The door banged shut.

"Mommy never lets me play with men, except Grandpa and Uncle Ron. She never leaves me with a man either. Since she left me with you, you must be my daddy."

Tony looked at Kelly.

"Yes, honey. Tony's your daddy."

Brett threw his arms around his neck and Tony finally gave him the hug and stopped fighting tears.

"I love you, son."

"But you just met me, Daddy."

"I love you just because you're my son. I loved you as soon as I saw you."

"I love you, Daddy. Are you going to live with us now?"

"Ah, no."

"But you can see your daddy almost every day. He only lives a few blocks away. How's that sound?"

"Yeah!"

***

Tony stayed well into the evening, knowing he would hear about it later, but not caring. He agreed to return after work on Monday. He walked home past the parsonage, hoping for a talk, but the pastor had guests. The next morning he dragged himself to work with very little sleep.

After feeding the horses, he found himself standing in front of the coffee pot, not knowing why. Don spoke close to his elbow.

"You must have seen the kid."

"You knew?"

"I knew that she listed her beneficiary as Brett Anthony, living at the same address, and she asked about schools."

"Why didn't you tell me?"

"It was none of my business. Did she hit you up for child support?"

"No. But I'll give it to her. That's my son, Don."

"You sure?"

"I'll show you my baby pictures some time. He's my son. He's great. He's smart. He figured out who I am."

"You're thrilled."

"Yeah."

"Well, good for you. Not everyone would feel that way."

"Why not?"

Don laughed.

"I guess you wouldn't understand. A lot of guys wouldn't want to be tied down. Wouldn't want the responsibility."

"No, I don't understand. I made him. Of course, I want the responsibility. And the joy. I've missed so much already. I don't think I could be happier."

"Except now everyone will know about your wild weekend."

"Oh, that. I don't care."

"Don't care? Who are you and what'd you do with the reverend?"

"I don't care, Don. I have a son. I want to shout it for everyone to hear. I'm ashamed of what I did. But Brett's a blessing. Something wonderful from the worst thing I ever did. I don't deserve him."

Don shook his head.

"You have the worst case of new father syndrome I've ever seen."

"He was like that all afternoon," Kelly said.

"You're pretty underhanded there, young lady."

She shrugged.

"A kid deserves to know his father."

"He's got a great one. Don't forget that."

"I know."

"But now he's got another distraction. He used to be so focused."

"I'll be better for it," Tony said. "And I want to change the beneficiary on my insurance."

"I suppose so. Come on."

***

After work, Tony walked past the parsonage and found Pastor Johnson working in his garden.

"Can I bend your ear for a few minutes?"

"If you don't mind talking while I work."

"I'll give you a hand. What should I do?"

"Rake the rows smooth before I plant. Was that your son in church yesterday?"

"Yeah. You're pretty smart."

"Almost everyone wondered when you hurried across the street. I had the advantage of our previous conversation. He looks like you."

"He really does. I can't believe how happy I am. I don't deserve such a blessing."

"That's why they're called blessings. We don't deserve any of them. But this rules out keeping your past between you, me, and the Lord."

"I know. When I couldn't sleep last night, I wrote a letter to the congregation."

He pulled a folded paper from his pocket.

"Read it to me."

"Members of St. Paul's. Before I entered the seminary, I did some things which I'm not proud of. These I have shared with my spiritual advisors. The Lord in his wisdom, has chosen to bless me despite my human weaknesses. Last Sunday I learned that I have a 5-year-old son. I feel truly blessed to be given something so wonderful. I want to spend as much time with him as I can. I apologize to the congregation if this reflects badly on our church."

"Satisfactory. Would you like me to print that in next Sunday's bulletin?"

"I'd appreciate that. I'll have to work."

"It seems that a weight has been lifted from you."

"I don't have to keep a secret anymore. I guess I really wanted to remind everyone that I'm imperfect just like everyone else."

"They shouldn't need reminding, but I believe certain people did put you on a pedestal."

"I'm afraid dating is out for a while. I want to spend that time with my son."

"And his mother."

"I'll spend a lot of time with her too. But I'll take Brett sometimes, so she can have time for herself. She's been doing this alone for a couple years."

"Just be on guard, Tony. You've strayed with this woman before. The temptation will be there."

"Thanks, I'm aware of that. It's never far from my mind."

***

"Evergreen One, this is Evergreen Five," Tony spoke into the pickup's radio.

Don replied quickly.

"Go ahead, Five."

"I have a late hiker. He said in his registration that he'd be back Monday afternoon. He was taking the Sky Line trail."

"Alone?"

"Yeah. I warned him."

"Almost a day late. You and Kelly get some horses. Ride up that way. I'll send Kevin and Red up Lava Flow, in case he decided to come back the easier way."

"What about your bulletin on missing hikers?"

"Let's just wait until you check the trails before we sound any false alarms."

"Okay."

"I'll have Kelly saddle the horses while you're on your way here. What's the macho man's name?"

"Ted Richards, from California by his license plates."

When he reached headquarters he found Kelly leading the horses to the trailer. He double-checked equipment. She had remembered everything. They loaded the horses and headed back to the trail head.

"Have you ever done searches?" he asked.

"Yeah. But it was easier in the Badlands. You could get on top of a butte and see for miles with binoculars. We found most of them that way."

"That would be nice. These searches have been known to last weeks. There are records of people who've never been found. Always some tough guy who didn't need a hiking partner."

"Don said you talked to this guy?"

"Yeah. I warned him. But he was used to getting his own way."

He climbed out and opened an access gate that would gain them two extra miles on the trail before they would need the horses. He closed it behind them, then directed Kelly to their parking spot. While they unloaded and prepared to mount, he told her about the trail.

"We can't make the whole thing on horseback. The last half-mile is too steep or too narrow. We'll have to hike it."

"Don said we won't make it back tonight."

"Not this late in the day. Does Brett know?"

"I called him. He was a little worried until I told him you'd be with me."

"Ha! You're as good at this as I am."

"But you're a daddy. I'm just a mommy. Guess that makes a difference to a little boy."

"Let's go. When we get into the dense forest, we need to keep quiet, stop, and listen."

"What about bears?"

"The bells on the horses warn bears that we're coming."

"Okay."

***

They followed the trail, listening for a person in distress, scanning with binoculars any time they had a view. They reached the end of the horse trail about two hours before sunset. Tony called Don on a portable radio.

"We're about to take to our feet. So far, nothing."

"Kevin and Red have already been to Eagle's Roost and are on their way back. Nothing that way either. Be careful up there."

"Always."

"Will the horses stay put with hobbles?" Kelly asked.

"They'll stay in this meadow because they can't negociate the trail home in hobbles. But sometimes we end up with a little hike. We hobble instead of tie because they have a better chance if a bear comes around. We'll camp here tonight."

"With bears."

"They don't spend much time at this elevation. We shouldn't have to worry about that. Let's go. I don't want to negociate this trail after dark."

They leaned against a rock face on their right, watching where they placed their feet on the twenty inch wide trail. On their left, a nearly vertical drop about the height of a ten-story building. The trail widened after a hundred yards, moving away from the precipice. Kelly let her breath out.

"Remind me not to come this way unless I have to."

"Amen."

The remainder of the Sky Line trail required climbing with both hands and feet. They crested the last ridge and looked down on a meadow in an ancient volcanic crater. When he pointed out mountain goats on the far rim, she smiled.

"Cool. I guess I'd come here again on the easier trail."

They both used their binoculars, seeing no sign of the missing hiker. Climbing back down the steepest section of the trail proved the toughest part of their day. The second time along the cliff trail required less nerve on Kelly's part. They found the horses grazing on the lush grass only a few feet from where they had left them. Tony radioed Don again, while Kelly began unsaddling. They rolled out their sleeping bags just as the sun dipped behind the mountains.

"What did you pack for supper?" Tony asked.

"The packages said beef stew."

"The MRE beef stew's pretty good. I'll heat some water."

He put together a one-burner camp stove while she emptied the contents of the stew packages on plates. While they waited for the water to boil, she gazed at the western sky.

"This is beautiful. I think I'm getting used to the elevation."

"We're a lot higher than Spruce Lake. Close to 8000 feet."

She yawned.

"Is that why I'm so tired?"

"Probably. But we worked hard today."

"I'm glad Don sent me with you."

"Now that we're past the last part of the trail, I am too."

"Did you worry about me?"

"I worried about Brett, with both his parents walking along the edge of a cliff."

"Oh. Glad I didn't think of that." Tony poured water into the plates and in short order they wolfed down the stew. "You're right. That was good."

He cleaned his plate with bread.

"What's for dessert?"

"Candy bars of some kind."

"Remember the first time I offered you a candy bar?"

Kelly grinned.

"I threatened to kill you if you didn't hand it over. If we snuggle tonight, will you react the same as you did back then."

"No-o. I'm not a hormone-addicted teenager anymore."

"Good. Because I'll bet it's going to get cold tonight. Can we zip these sleeping bags together?"

"Ye-es."

"Come on now. You said you could handle it."

"I did, didn't I. Maybe I spoke too soon. I haven't had the chance to test that theory."

"Nobody since me?"

"Nothing intimate. No."

"You really *did* feel guilty, didn't you."

"Yeah."

"Eventually I did too. Want to know the real reason I used you like that?" He shrugged. "To get even with my boyfriend. A couple weeks before the end of the semester, a friend told me that he'd been cheating on me the whole time we were separated. He couldn't even stay faithful to me for a couple months at a time. We'd talked about marriage. I thought it'd just serve him right if I had another guy's baby. A complete stranger was even better."

Tony tried to suppress a smile.

"You know that's really dumb, don't you?"

"Well, yeah. I blame it on that woman scorned thing. I was so mad I wasn't thinking straight."

"I see. I'll tie the horses for the night. You work on those sleeping bags."

When he returned, she had already climbed in. He placed a rifle beside the bags and removed his boots before joining her. He tensed when she melted against him. She ignored it.

"Oh, I forgot how good a hard body feels. You were the last for me too, you know."

"Really? You did learn something."

"That's what I've been trying to tell you."

***

When they woke the next morning, frost covered their sleeping bag. Kelly looked around, then snuggled against Tony's chest and covered her head.

"We can just stay in here a while longer, can't we."

"We'll wait until the sun hits us. We can't ride across frosty rocks anyhow."

"That wouldn't be safe at all."

"Maybe this isn't either."

"You done good so far."

"But I'm wide awake now."

"Me too. And you feel awfully good."

Her fingers found an opening between the buttons of his shirt. He gasped.

"Don't."

She withdrew her hand and poked her head out.

"I'm sorry. I'm feeling playful. I really don't want to seduce you. But with our history, you take everything that way. I can't blame you."

"It's not that I don't trust you."

"Yes, it is."

"Well, it's not just that. I don't trust myself. I'm afraid I'll turn into the buck in rutt again."

"You just don't have enough experience. The only way you've ever handled an affectionate woman is with sex."

"Affectionate, huh?"

"You've never slept with a woman unless it involved sex."

"No. I didn't think that was possible."

"So you think married couples do it every night."

"I guess not. I suppose I'm pretty naive."

"Yeah. But that's kind of endearing."

He sighed.

"I miss Brett."

"Me too."

"I don't see how I can go back to school this fall."

"Whoa! Kind of early to worry about that. Just enjoy the time you can spend with him. Let God take care of next fall."

"Good advice. I'd better turn the horses loose so they can graze. Did you pack some hot chocolate?"

"Yeah. That sounds good. I'll just wait here until it's ready."

She grinned.

"Okay. No reason both of us should be cold."

"You're such a gentleman."

They ate breakfast, then saddled the horses. Tony decided that the rocks were still too wet to ride. They led their mounts down the trail. Sunny locations dried quickly, but shaded spots remained frosty. Finally, they reached a point where the trail consisted of more dirt and pine needles than rock.

"We should be able to ride from here."

He tightened his cinch.

"Tony, is this blood?"

He dropped the reins and looked where she pointed. The rust-colored dead pine needles and dead leaves camouflaged the dried blood.

"Yeah. A lot of it. A blood trail like you'd see with a wounded animal. It's disturbed. We must have ridden right through it yesterday." The large drops crossed their trail. He walked to the right and noticed that the drops pointed in the opposite direction. "It was moving that way. Tie the horses away from the blood trail and bring your rifle."

He took his and followed the blood.

"Could it be human?"

Tony sighed and pointed to a track in the dirt, a hiking boot rimmed with blood. Neither of them said another word. He saw evidence that the injured person had been running. They both noticed the large, disturbed spot in the pine needles and a substantial blood stain, then the trail continued. The tracks ended in a large pool of dried blood, but no body.

"He bled out here."

"Oh, God. Poor guy. Bear tracks!"

"And drag marks." They both checked their guns before following the drag marks. Soon, they heard the unmistakable grunts of a bear. He raised his rifle and crept forward until they saw the black bear feeding on a human body. "If I don't drop her, empty your gun into her."

Kelly nodded. The sow raised her head and Tony fired. She roared and rose on her hind legs. His second shot dropped her. He lowered his rifle with trembling hands, then waited a moment before advancing. He put another bullet into the bear's skull at point blank range.

"Better safe than sorry."

"Yeah. Do I hear a baby crying?"

Tony listened, then nodded.

"More than one."

He walked around the dead bear with Kelly at his heels. A short search of the bushes yielded two frightened cubs, just old enough to follow their mother.

"Oh-h. They sound almost human."

"Yeah. Stay here with them. Get them used to your scent. I'll radio Don and get instructions. We found our missing hiker."

"What if they run away?"

"They won't."

"You're sure this is our guy?"

"I recognize what's left of his clothes."

"Oh."

Tony walked half-way back to the horses before headquarters picked up his radio signal.

"You find something?" Don asked.

"The subject of our search, deceased."

"A fall?"

"No. A bear got to him before we did, but cause of death appears to be homicide."

A pause.

"Someone wants to talk to you. Answer his questions."

An unfamiliar voice with a slight drawl replaced Don's.

"What makes you think that?"

"Bears don't carry guns. Multiple gunshot wounds."

"Don't disturb anything. How close can we land a chopper?"

Tony thought about the terrain.

"About a quarter mile."

"Tell your boss your location and stay there."

Tony relayed the information to Don. "There's a meadow along the trail about a quarter mile below our location. One of us will meet the chopper and guide them here. We need transport for two bear cubs."

"Will do. I'll send Red up with a pack horse. You two okay?"

"Yeah. Maybe a little shaky."

"Hang in there."

"Don't have much choice."

He signed off and walked back to Kelly. She sat on the ground while the cubs approached her, jumping back, then advancing again. He kept his distance to avoid scaring them.

"Don had me talk to someone who might have been an FBI agent. They're flying a helicopter up here. I don't know how long it will take to arrange that. I told them where to land, but one of us needs to meet them."

She spoke quietly, but even so, the cubs recoiled.

"I'll meet them. Staying here with that body is creeping me out."

"Okay. But I'll ask you to stay here a little longer. I'll move the horses to that patch of grass we crossed just before we found the blood. Then I'll point you to the landing site. Red's bringing a pack horse to haul the babies down."

"What will we do with them?"

"That's what the pens behind headquarters are for. These guys are small enough someone will have to do a nighttime feeding for a while."

"Who gets that honor?"

"Whoever does night patrols."

"What happens when they grow up?"

"Probably a zoo. I'd better move the horses."

"I'll be here."

***

Tony resisted the urge to back track the blood trail, knowing they had already contaminated the crime scene enough. He directed Kelly to the landing site, then sat with the cubs. Having become accustomed to human scent, they warmed up to him faster than they had to Kelly.

He avoided looking at either body. An hour passed. By the time he heard the helicopter, the cubs were curled up with their heads on his thighs. He saw no reason to disturb them by standing to meet the expected law officers. Before long, they followed Kelly across the rise. Ryan and two guys in FBI jackets. The agents cast skeptical glances at him before one began taking pictures and the other pulled on latex gloves. Ryan crouched beside Tony.

"Baby sitting?"

"I made them orphans."

"Had to. We can't have a man eater running around. Even if she didn't kill him, she got a taste for it. Besides, these guys want to see what's in her stomach."

"There's a great thought. How long will this take?"

"God only knows. The few murders I've handled, either the killer waited for us to get there, or there were a pile of witnesses who knew the killer by name. Glad we had these guys on board from the get go."

"Yeah."

"They'll be asking you some questions. Just give them the facts as you know them."

"I know. I had the peace officer training."

He and Kelly waited with the cubs while Ryan retraced the trail, placing markers for the photographer. The other agent finally pointed at

Tony.

"Come with me," he said. Tony extracted himself from the cubs and followed the agent until they were out of hearing range from Kelly. "Start from the beginning. Just tell me what you saw."

"We rode through here yesterday, but didn't see anything. There was frost this morning, so we led our horses down from the higher elevations. When we got to the trail over there, I decided it was safe to ride. Kelly spotted the blood when we were getting ready to mount. I've tracked wounded animals. That's what it looked like. I started off to the right, but noticed the blood drops pointed this way."

"Pointed?"

"Yeah. Directionality."

"You know about that?"

"I took a class."

The agent's thick, black eyebrows nearly met.

"Amateur detective?"

"No. Peace officer training."

"Go on."

"We tied the horses and followed the blood trail. We found a boot print, with blood around it. We saw where he fell. There was quite a bit of blood there. He got up again, and a little farther on we saw the last place he fell. From the amount of blood, he must have bled out there. We saw bear tracks and followed the drag marks here. At that point, I thought the bear could have killed him, so I shot the bear."

"What did you do next?"

"I made sure the bear was dead. I recognized the clothes on the victim."

"You'd seen him before?"

"I was there when he started up this trail."

"We'll get back to that. What else did you notice?"

"Gunshot wounds in the arm that wasn't eaten and both legs. There's no sign of his backpack. His watch is missing. And a ring. That was gone too."

The agent fixed an icy gaze on him.

"You're pretty observant. What did you notice when you met him?"

"His equipment was all top of the line. The watch was expensive, a Rolex or something. He had a ring on his left hand and two on the right hand. A gold chain around his neck. With a number one on it. He seemed to be a risk-taker. When he asked about the trails, I told him that we don't recommend people hike this alone. He resisted when I asked him to fill out the hiker registration."

"I saw the form. You must have convinced him."

"I explained that we didn't want to start looking for him if he was planning to be gone a couple weeks. He saw the wisdom of that."

"Did you see anyone who may have been watching him?"

"No. There was no one else around. Just three other vehicles in the lot . . ."

"What else?"

"We had forms from two hiking parties and one on horseback. But just before I got back to the lot, I met a lone hiker. He said he'd filled out a registration form, but there wasn't another one for a single hiker."

"Did he carry a pack big enough to hold a rifle?"

"If it was broken down."

"Describe him."

"In his thirties. Sandy hair. Moustache. About six feet. A big man. Rugged. He wore a baseball cap and aviator glasses, so I don't know about his eyes. When he walked away from me I noticed that he had a bumper sticker on his backpack from Yellowstone. The pack was olive drab."

"M-m. So he probably saw the victim in the parking lot?"

"Most likely."

"What day was this?"

"Friday."

"What time was this?"

"A little after ten."

"Okay. Stay here. I'm going to talk to your partner."

Tony waited until he walked away, then sank to a boulder. Kelly rose to meet the agent. He addressed her in a very different tone than he had used with Tony.

"Ma'am, I'm Agent Garret. You are?"

"Kelly Thiel."

"Your boss told me you're pretty new here."

"Three weeks."

"So Wagner was in charge on this assignment?"

"Yes."

"Tell me what happened."

"We rode up Sky Line trail looking for that hiker. We went as far as we could on horseback, then hiked the rest of the way up to Eagle's Roost. We got back to the horses just before dark, and camped there. This morning it was frosty. Tony decided that it was too dangerous to ride on frost-covered rocks, so we led the horses."

"Did you agree with him?"

"After I thought about it, yeah."

"Go on."

"We led the horses until Tony decided it was safe to ride."

"Was that a good place to mount, or did you think you could have been riding sooner?"

Kelly frowned.

"I thought maybe we could have been riding sooner, but I grew up in North Dakota. What do I know about mountains?"

"I understand."

"When I picked up my reins, I saw the blood. Tony walked a few feet, then said the trail went the other way. We moved the horses. Tony showed me the track. I was scared, but Tony stayed so calm. We followed the trail until we found where the guy bled out. I spotted the bear tracks. The drag marks were easy to follow. Tony told me if he didn't drop the bear, I should empty my rifle into her. He got off two shots before I could pull my trigger."

"What did you notice about the body?"

"Blood. I didn't look at it. I was trying not to lose my breakfast."

"How did Wagner handle it?"

"I think he was a little shaky. But he just kept doing what he needed to do. He was kind of inspirational. Why all the questions about Tony?"

"I asked him the same questions about you?"

"Oh."

"Anything else to add?"

"Not that I can think of."

"Thank you, ma'am. If you think of anything else, let me know."

Kelly rejoined Tony with the bear cubs at her heels. They each sat holding a cub while Garret returned to the body.

"How you doing?" She asked.

He shrugged.

"I've had better days."

"Yeah. I just want to go home and go to bed."

"I hear you."

"I wonder when we'll get to do that."

"Tonight, if we're lucky."

"Wonderful."

***

No one told them what the agents found at the other end of the blood trail. When Red arrived, the FBI recruited all of them to help carry the hiker and the bear to the helicopter. Agent Garret told them he would be waiting at park headquarters when they returned.

With the cubs secured on a pack horse accustomed to such unusual cargo, the three rangers rode down the mountain, reaching the trail head in gathering darkness. They found park headquarters brightly illuminated, but the lot so full they could barely drive in. Don met them by the stable.

"Red, feed those cubs. The pen's ready. You two, unsaddle the horses, then come inside."

They nodded and followed orders. Kelly sought out Don in the crowd of FBI agents.

"I need to call Brett."

"Go ahead if you can find a phone."

She nudged aside an agent and took her cell phone from her desk. Tony followed her to the ranger sleeping room while she called. Her sitter put Brett on the phone.

"Mommy, I've been worried about you."

"We've been really busy at work, honey. We just got back to the office."

"Are you coming home now?"

"I don't know, honey. We have some paper work to do. It might be late."

"Daddy has paper work too?"

"Yes. Would you like to talk to him?"

"Yeah."

"Here he is."

"Hi, son."

"Hi, Daddy. Are you and Mommy okay?"

"Just tired."

"You'd better go to bed."

"Good idea. We'll do that as soon as we can. I love you, son."

"Love you, Daddy."

He handed the phone back to Kelly and flopped on one of the beds. The rest of her conversation did not register. He dozed off before a loud voice woke him.

"Wagner!"

"Huh?"

"Come with me," a new face said.

Feeling disoriented, Tony looked around, recognized the room and noticed Kelly sleeping in another bed. He turned out the light as he left. The agent led him to Don's office, where Agent Garret waited. He motioned to a chair, which Tony gladly occupied.

"Do you own a key ring made by Gil Simon?"

Tony's mind refused to comprehend the question for a moment.

"Everybody in town does. And most of the tourists who've ever been here."

"Let's see yours."

Tony had to think about its location.

"Okay. It's in my desk." An agent followed him there and back. "It's broke. I lost the antler part."

He saw the agents exchange glances. Garret's brows nearly met again. He reached into a box and pulled out an evidence bag containing a carved antler. Tony leaned forward. It looked like the antler which had been attached to his key ring. *That doesn't make sense.*

"Where'd you find that?"

"Where you lost it. Would you like to amend your story about your movements after you found the blood trail?"

"No. And I didn't even have my keys with me. I leave them in my desk. One of your guys was sitting there when we got back. He'll tell you I didn't go near it."

"Then explain to me how this ended up where the victim was initially shot."

Tony sat trying to explain that to himself, before admitting his confusion out loud.

"I don't know."

"That's not good enough."

"It could belong to someone else. Gil only makes about four designs."

"There are partial prints on this one. We'll compare them to yours soon enough."

"Okay."

"Will you submit a DNA sample?"

"Yeah. Can I get some sleep now?"

"Hellfire, Wagner. A man's dead and you're worried about *sleep*."

"I'm not used to finding bodies. You flew up there and back in a helicopter. I rode a horse both ways! I'm so tired I can't think straight!"

"Okay. After they collect your DNA, you can go to one of the bunks in the back."

"Thank you."

***

Rough hands dragged Tony from the bed and he found his arms cuffed behind his back before he woke fully. He thought about protesting, but Kelly beat him to it.

"What the heck are you doing?"

"Just stay out of it, ma'am," an agent said.

"No, I won't stay out of it. Why are you treating him like a suspect?"

"Because he is a suspect, ma'am."

"That's ludicrous. Don! Can you talk sense to them?"

She followed the agents with Tony. Don's red face contrasted sharply with his white beard. He glared at agent Garret.

"I tried to tell the idiot! Anyone in town would make a better suspect than Tony. Hell, I'm more likely to kill somebody. Tony, keep your mouth shut. Tell 'em you want a lawyer. I'll send someone."

"You're impeding an investigation, Storm," Garret said.

Don snorted.

"You're wasting your time on an innocent man. So that makes you the one impeding the investigation."

Tony felt dizzy. *Suspect? I'm a suspect? They think I could kill somebody like that?* The agents shoved him into the back seat of a car and left town. *How could they think that?* The agent in the passenger seat read him his Miranda rights.

"Do you understand these rights?"

"Yeah. Yeah. I guess so."

The car turned south in the dark. The clock on the dash read 4:20. He became acutely aware of his arms behind his back. *And I'm not wearing a seat belt. There are a lot of deer through here.* His concern suddenly struck him as funny and he laughed out loud. The agent stared at him. *This whole ordeal is crazy.* Tony could not stop laughing. *They must think I'm insane.*

"Knock it off!"

"I'm sorry. It must be sleep deprivation."

"Go to sleep then."

"I'll try."

Tony lay on the seat. Too uncomfortable to sleep, he continued to giggle off and on until the car stopped. He sat up, noticing that they were in a city, in a parking lot with numerous highway patrol and police cars. The driver dragged him from the car and prodded him along to a building.

After passing through two doors, they waited for a third to slide open. When it closed, they removed his handcuffs. He loosened his shoulders.

"Empty your pockets. Remove your outer clothes and shoes."

He followed orders, no longer amused. A man in uniform gave him an orange jumpsuit and slippers. The same man took his finger prints and pictures, then asked for his name, address, and a few other questions. Tony answered them, seeing nothing incriminating in the information. Then they left him alone in an interrogation room. He rested his head on his arms on the table.

He woke to the sound of Glen Roberts swearing.

"I need some time to confer with my client."

Tony raised his head. Glen wore a suit jacket over faded jeans and a t-shirt.

"Hi, Glen."

"You look like hell."

"So do you."

"Don called me at four a.m. When I finished cussing him out, he filled me in. I got dressed in a hurry. Before I left the house, Ryan called. He said he was taking up a collection to pay my fee."

"That's awful nice of him."

"You've done enough nice things for other people. The town will be ready to lynch FBI agents when they hear about this. Have they told you the charges?"

"No. But they think I killed that hiker."

"I talked to Don on the drive down here. The guy had to be killed between Friday morning at ten and Tuesday afternoon when you rode up the trail. The horses definitely walked through the blood trail on the way up. We need to account for your whereabouts that whole time."

"I worked until four on Friday, mowed Ethel's lawn and had supper with her Friday evening. Saturday morning, I left early on a hike. I didn't get home till almost one."

"Did anybody see you?"

"No. I avoid people when I hike."

"That's bad. Go on."

"In the afternoon, I tilled Anna Hathaway's garden. I had supper alone and read a book. Sunday morning, I ushered at church."

"And?"

"Sunday afternoon and evening I spent with my son."

"Your *son*?"

"Yeah. Didn't know I had one until Sunday."

"You've had quite a week."

"No kidding. Monday I worked."

"So the only time you really don't have an alibi is from Friday night until Saturday at 1:00. That would technically give you time to do the deed. Hopefully, they can narrow down the time of death to exclude you, but I understand that body's in pretty tough shape."

"Yeah."

"What makes them suspect you?"

"You know those key rings Gil makes?" Glen nodded. "I lost the antler off mine. They found one like it at the initial crime scene. But they must have something else. That just got them interested."

"Everybody in town has those key rings." Agent Garret entered and dropped a file on the table. "I'm Glen Roberts, representing Mr. Wagner. What are the charges against my client?"

"He's being held as a material witness in the murder of Ted Richards."

"He's an upstanding member of the community. No flight risk. Release him to my custody."

"He's a summer employee, with no permanent ties to the community."

"Because he's a seminary student the rest of the year."

"Seminary?"

"Yeah."

"We're not releasing him."

"Then you'd better tell me what you got."

"We have Mr. Wagner's finger prints on a carved chunk of antler found at the site where Richards was first shot."

"He admits losing it. Anyone could have planted it there."

"Convenient. Last night, we executed a search warrant for his apartment and the property it stands on, which led us to what appears to be the murder weapon, hidden in the woods behind his apartment."

"I understand your basis for a warrant to search his apartment. But his landlord's property? You know that won't stand up in court."

"Oh, I think it will. We received an anonymous tip that we could find the weapon there."

"Anyone could have put it there. Probably the anonymous tipster."

"We found Mr. Wagner's hair on the gun."

Tony knew better.

"You couldn't have DNA results yet. You have no proof that's my hair."

"We will soon. We've put a rush on it. It's the right color."

"Now he's guilty because he's blond. If that's the case you could arrest our sheriff too."

"We didn't find the sheriff's prints at the crime scene or the murder weapon near his residence."

Glen waved a hand.

"Circumstantial. That DNA test will take at least another 24 hours. My client is innocent until proven guilty, not the other way around."

"We have enough evidence to hold your client."

"When was Richards killed?"

"The medical examiner still has the body."

"My client has people who can swear to his whereabouts for most of this weekend. He is not available for questioning until you have a TOD. In the meantime, he's suffering from sleep deprivation. If he isn't fed and allowed to sleep, I'm calling a judge."

Garret gathered his folder and left the room. Tony sighed.

"Will that work?"

"Should. If they don't let you sleep, I can challenge anything you say during questioning. I'm going back to Spruce Lake. And you aren't talking without me here. Understand?"

"Yeah."

"Just let them give you room and board for a day. We'll get you out of this. I'd sure like to know who's trying to frame you. Nobody would buy you as a murderer."

"The FBI does."

"M-m. Try not to worry."

"If I start to worry, I'll just pray."

***

Exhaustion allowed Tony to sleep in the noisy jail. When he woke in the afternoon, he heard other prisoners talking about a crowd in the parking lot. He leaned on the bars of his cell door to hear more.

"Hey, you Tony?" Another prisoner asked.

"Yeah. Why?"

"Your fan club's in the parking lot."

"Fan club?"

"They got a whole school bus full of people out there, protesting your incarceration. There's some with signs calling the FBI stupid. What'd you do?"

"Nothing. That's the problem."

"Same here. What they accusing you of?"

"Murder."

"Big time! You should have plenty of character witnesses. Good luck."

Tony sighed and thanked God for his friends. He thought of Brett and hoped that he could see him soon. A guard came to his door.

"You have a visitor."

"Oh. Who?"

"Your boss. This way."

The guard took him to a room where plexiglass separated him from Don.

"How you doing, reverend?"

"I'm not so tired. Did you come on the bus?"

"You heard about that. I drove myself. That's mostly little old ladies and housewives. Nobody in town is answering the FBI's questions. They all agreed to give the same answer, 'When you release Tony, we'll talk.' Bet Garret's fit to be tied."

"Would you thank everybody out there for me?"

"Course."

"How's Kelly and Brett?"

"She's worried about you. I gave her today off, but she called twice. She's trying to keep this from Brett without lying to him. She's a good gal. Glad to have her on our team."

"Yeah. Why would somebody try to frame me?"

"Whoever it is couldn't know you. They must have seen you that day you talked to Richards. They decided you'd make a good patsy."

"But where'd he get my key ring?"

"I don't have an answer for that one. Maybe he saw you drop it somewhere and decided to frame you then. You meeting Richards was just gravy. Do you remember when you lost it?"

"No. I had it when I came back to town. I haven't driven my car since. I don't lock my apartment door. I'm not sure why I even brought the keys to work. They've been in my desk for a week."

"So somebody could have taken it from your desk. Although I hate to think that anyone who works for me could have done this."

"Sometimes we get visitors. If a pair came in and distracted the person on duty, they could have searched a desk or two."

"Possible. I'll ask everyone if anything like that happened."

"Thanks."

"I called your folks this morning."

"Did you have to?"

"Yeah. I think I did. This could make national news. You want 'em to find out that way?"

"No. How'd they take it?"

"About like the rest of us. I convinced them not to come right out. I'll call them again tonight. Glen says he should be able to get you out tomorrow."

"Just keep Mom and Dad away from here. I haven't quite figured out how to tell them about Brett."

"I'll do the best I can. But the sooner you tell them, the better."

"I know. I just need to get used to it myself."

"True. Seems like weeks since Sunday."

"Tell me about it."

***

Glen and Agent Garret met Tony in the interrogation room. Garret showed them a DNA profile.

"This confirms that the hairs found with the gun are yours."

"People lose hair," Glen said. "I can pick up yours and plant it somewhere. You said you had TOD."

"The bear caused too much damage to get a real narrow window. Saturday or Sunday. However, the victim was still wearing a sophisticated GPS. It showed him reaching the point where he bled out at 4:30 Sunday afternoon."

Tony let his breath out.

"Thank God."

Glen explained.

"Tony was with his son from the time he left church on Sunday until well into the evening."

"Son? How old's his son?"

"Five," Tony said.

"And who's his mother?"

"Kelly Thiel."

"That's a suspect alibi."

"Ask her neighbors. I'm sure someone noticed me there. People notice me."

"They also trust you. We have a petition with more than three hundred signatures, demanding your release. We have another bus load of protestors in the parking lot today. Despite the evidence, I'm beginning to believe you're innocent. We'll release you while we check your alibi. Don't leave Spruce Lake. And we need to you to give a description of that hiker to a sketch artist."

"Okay. When?"

"Before you leave here."

Garret opened the door, called in the artist, and told a guard to release Tony. An hour later, Tony walked out the door with Glen. He grinned when the crowd cheered, then exchanged hugs with most.

"Thanks for being here for me. It means a lot."

"They got this foolishness out of their heads?" Clarice asked.

"They're coming around. They just need to check my alibi. You can all go home now."

"Good advice," Glen said. "I'll take Tony home so he can get some rest."

Tony followed him to his car.

"Thanks, Glen. I'd like to see my son before I go home."

"You can use my phone to call Kelly."

"Thanks."

***

"Daddy!"

Tony kneeled and hugged Brett.

"I missed you, son."

"Mommy said you helped the FBI."

"Yeah."

"She said a man died."

"Yes. That's pretty sad."

"Yeah. Will you help the FBI more?"

"Maybe. It was hard work. I'm going home to bed. But I wanted to see you first."

"Can I see you tomorrow?"

"I think so."

He stood and Kelly hugged him. She whispered.

"You okay?"

"Just tired."

"I'm glad you're home."

She kissed his cheek. He waved good bye and walked home.

When Betty saw him walk up the driveway, she ran out to hug him.

"Oh, honey, are you okay?"

"I'm fine, thanks."

Gil came from the garage.

"I leave for a few days and the town falls apart. Betty told me when I got home this morning that you're in jail and the FBI's been searching our property. I thought she'd lost her marbles."

"Everything seemed pretty insane for a while."

"Would you like some lunch?" Betty asked.

"No, thanks. I'll grab a bowl of cereal and hit the sack. But if anybody shows up looking for me, sic the dogs on them."

"We don't have dogs."

He smiled and kissed her forehead.

"Good night, Betty."

***

"What the heck you doing here, reverend?"

"I'm on the schedule today. You had to get along without me yesterday. Didn't want to strain your resources too much."

"You sure you're ready for it?"

"It's better if I don't have too much time to think. Did they confirm my alibi?"

"Kelly said there were more FBI agents than residents in her neighborhood late yesterday. Haven't heard what they found out."

"Where are they?"

"Sheriff's office. The whole town knows about your kid. That shock, on top of what already happened, just about did in a few old ladies."

"I suppose."

"And you'd better figure out how to tell your folks. They're on their way."

Tony groaned.

"How soon?"

"They were leaving this morning."

"Tomorrow afternoon. Did you try to change their minds?"

"I told them you're fine. They want to be sure."

"I guess it's better to get it over. Did you feed the cubs this morning?"

"First thing. They're good for a couple hours. I told Ryan we need a road kill deer to get them eating meat."

"What you want me to do?"

"You and Kelly check the campgrounds. I think that girl's sweet on you."

Tony made a face.

"She just cares about Brett's father, now that she's found him. Wonder what she'll think about meeting my parents."

"Meeting your parents!" Kelly said.

"Don couldn't convince them to stay home. They'll be here tomorrow."

"And I'm the woman who led their son astray."

"It's worse than you think. I never told them about you."

"Don, got a remote assignment for me tomorrow? I'll let them fall in love with Brett before they meet me."

"Trying to avoid your responsibility?"

"Yeah."

"Too bad."

***

When they returned from checking campgrounds, a federal car occupied the headquarters lot. They entered with reservations. Garret sat at a desk alone while Don pretended to work in his office. Garret rose.

"Wagner, good thing you live in a town full of busybodies. Some people saw you walk home with her. Some saw you there. And others saw you leave. Your alibi's good. Whoever tried to frame you didn't count on that."

"Thank God."

"Come with me." Tony followed him outside. "I operate under the assumption that everybody's a suspect until they've been cleared. As far as I'm concerned, you're the only innocent man in town. I need a guide I can trust. You willing to do it?"

"What did Don say?"

"He said if you want to spend time with the likes of me, he'll loan you out."

"You're sure about me?"

"Yeah."

"Okay."

"Tell him we're leaving. I have the chopper waiting."

"How long will we be gone? I promised my son I'd spend time with him after work."

"We'll be back before dark."

Tony informed Don and Kelly, then rode with Garret to the helicopter pad behind the sheriff's office. Another agent–Phillips--and the pilot waited there. Not wanting to look like a hick, Tony told no one this would be his first time in a helicopter. He gripped the door handle during take-off, then enjoyed the flight. He recognized a few landmarks, but admired the pilot's ability to find the same meadow.

Garret, Phillips, and Tony left the pilot and hiked to the place where they had found the body. Garret gave orders.

"We're going to spread out and back track along the trail. The killer followed him, probably enjoyed wounding him before finishing him off. But we haven't found any tracks. If we go off to the sides, maybe we'll find something. Wagner, you know what you're looking for?"

"I've done some tracking."

"If you even suspect you found anything, call me."

"Okay."

Tony walked slowly, searching every inch of the ground, stopping frequently to scan higher. When they crossed the hiking trail, Garret asked for a report before they continued. Unfamiliar with the direction now,

Tony tried to maintain his distance from Garret.

Still, they found nothing. Garret called them to a taped off area, the initial crime scene. His brows had crept together again.

"How can someone leave no signs? Do I need to get an Indian out here?"

"Maybe that's it," Tony said.

"An Indian did this. Give me a break."

"No. Someone in moccasins who knew his way around the wilderness."

Garret pulled at his ear.

"Hellfire. Better theory than I came up with. Richards' stuff's still missing. Let's make some assumptions. He had Richards drop his belongings here. Richards ran and was wounded. The unsub leaves the stuff, tracks him down, and kills him. Then he comes back and takes the stuff, not wanting to stick around to sort through it. But if he's smart, he'll get rid of the excess before he gets back to civilization. Tony, if you wanted to get out of here on foot without being seen, where would you go?"

Tony thought about the terrain, then pointed.

"That way. You can see how steep the slopes are the other way."

"Let's go. Spread out again. Maybe he got sloppy after he left the scene. What color was Richards' backpack?"

"Red. There are cliffs this way. He could have thrown over what he didn't want."

"If he did, it'll take more than the three of us to find it."

They used the same method to search this area. Tony stayed closest to the cliffs, though the solid rock provided no surface for tracks. *Yeah. This is where I'd go if I didn't want to be found.* When a point of rock jutted beyond the rest of the cliffs, he stopped and scanned the base of the cliffs with binoculars.

"You're falling behind, Wagner."

"I'm looking for the backpack."

"Good thinking."

They waited for him to catch up, then continued their slow progress. Something shiny caught Tony's eye. He crouched to inspect it. *Looks like a match container, a fancy one.*

"Over here!"

Garret and Phillips hurried to his location. Phillips took pictures and recorded the coordinates using a GPS. Garret collected the object in an evidence bag and examined it.

"There's an R engraved on it. Good job, Wagner. You know what it is?"

"A waterproof match container, I think. Most people use a pill bottle."

"It's a reasonable assumption that it belonged to our victim. We'll close our spacing and move on."

Tony used another point to survey the cliff face. Garret joined him, searching with his binoculars as well. Tony rubbed his eyes.

"You have many cases in this kind of country?"

"Not many. Though my specialty is rural crime. I've investigated three by this national park killer now."

"It's the same guy?"

"Everything's the same. We probably would have cleared you even without your alibi. I doubt you were in all the other parks at the time of the murders."

"There are more than three?"

"A lot more. There." He pointed. "Do you see something red down there?"

Tony first searched with his eyes, but saw nothing. With binoculars and Garret's guidance, it still took him some time to locate the patch of red.

"Looks like a backpack to me. It's caught on something. It must be a hundred feet from both the top and bottom."

"Let's get a GPS on it first." He spoke into his radio. "Phillips, walk along the cliff until I tell you to stop, then take a GPS reading."

"Yes, sir."

"Tony, can you get down there?"

"Did you bring climbing equipment?"

"Don't know." He spoke into the radio again. "Mc Kay, you got any climbing equipment in your chopper?" A long pause. "I probably caught him napping."

"Yeah. For one."

He looked at Tony.

"Do you climb?"

"Part of the job."

"Phillips, stop there. Call that reading to Mc Kay. Mc Kay, hoof it to Phillips location with the climbing equipment. Let's go, Tony."

When they reached Phillips, Tony lay on his belly to peer over the precipice. He could not see the backpack. *No surprise.*

"Hope we have enough rope."

"Here comes Mc Kay now."

Tony opened the duffle bag, finding harness, hardware, rope, and even a helmet. He squinted at the rope and began recoiling it.

"It'll be close."

"That won't get you all the way to the bottom?"

Tony chuckled.

"Bottom. I don't know if it'll get me to the backpack."

"I don't see any of those climby things. How you getting back up?"

"With your help. Unless you want to come back tomorrow with better equipment."

"Can you do this without getting yourself killed?"

"If I can't reach it, I won't do anything foolish. I'll come back without it."

"Okay."

"Once I get over the edge, I'll be able to see if I have enough rope. I won't have to go all the way down to figure it out."

"How you plan to bring it up?"

"Put it over my shoulder."

"Afraid not. Phillips, give him a bag. You need to bag it before you bring it up."

"You've got to be kidding. I won't have a free hand to carry a bag. Give me your belt."

Gibson complied. Tony tucked it and the bag into his own belt and pulled on the gloves he always carried. He tied the rope off to a sturdy tree and threw the rest over the rim. He hooked himself to the rope and leaned against it, backing over the edge. The cliff had a wide lip, forcing him to descend twenty feet before he could see the backpack.

"Bring me up." He walked up while they pulled. "I don't have enough rope to be safe and we need to go another thirty feet that way."

"Damn. First thing in the morning?"

"Yeah. I'll bring my own equipment."

"Good. We have another hour of daylight. We'll search another half-hour, then get back to the chopper."

***

The next morning, gray clouds obscured the sun when Garret picked up Tony and his equipment at headquarters.

"Can you do this if it rains?"

"Not me. Someone else might be crazy enough to try it."

"Well, let's hope it doesn't rain."

"I brought a bag and line to haul up the backpack. I'll have enough to do. And I brought the 'climby things' so you don't have to haul me up."

"Good. I don't like to work that hard."

As the helicopter ascended, the clouds grew closer. The pilot took an indirect route, sticking to valleys to avoid shrouded peaks. Tony worried that their landing site would be obscured. After flying through a few thin clouds, the chopper touched down on target.

Everyone hurried, recognizing that rain could start at any time. When they reached the cliff, Tony secured the rope to a tree and prepared to descend. He purposefully checked all his equipment. Hurry had no place when a mistake meant a two hundred foot fall.

"Keep the cargo line about twenty feet to the side of my rope. When I have the backpack in the netting, I'll tug on the line three times. Pull it up so it's out of my way."

"Got that, Phillips?"

Phillips nodded and Tony backed over the cliff. He had made more difficult climbs, but never requiring a task while hanging a hundred feet above the ground. He worked his way down the even cliff face, frequently checking his distance to the backpack. Just above it, he stopped to assess the situation.

If I'm not careful, I'll knock it off. One of the backpack's straps had caught on a rock wedged in a crevice. A strong wind could dislodge it. He moved to the side before descending perpendicular to the pack. He secured his rope and removed the netting and sack from his belt. He opened the sack, then sidled closer to the backpack.

Got it. After shoving the backpack inside, he sealed the sack, then deposited it in the netting. He tied that shut for safe keeping and tugged three times. More than a hundred feet of cargo line fell from the cliff. He watched in disbelief, gripping the netting. Expletives found their way to his tongue but never quite escaped.

"Sorry Lord."

Twenty pounds of dead weight would only make his climb more difficult. He tied the line around his shoulder and across his chest. Carefully removing his pocket knife, he cut the excess and let if fall. He replaced his knife before fastening the aiders to his rope. He slipped his feet into the stirrups and began the slow climb.

He needed several rest stops. During one of those, he smiled to himself. Phillips must have gotten an earful from Garret when he dropped that line. Garret had no qualms about using expletives. *Rain!* Not much, but enough to make him nervous. He pushed on, not resting as the rain came harder. His arms and legs protested. His lungs reminded him of the elevation.

By the time he came over the rim, a steady rain had developed. The FBI agents pulled him the last few feet. He lay on the rock, exhausted while Garret slapped him on the back.

"You got it! I was afraid we'd lost it when this moron dropped the rope."

Tony nodded.

"I almost . . . swore."

Garret laughed.

"We'll collect this stuff while you catch your breath."

Without getting up, Tony began extricating himself from the rope, then his climbing gear. He removed his helmet and sat up. The exhaustion and rain reminded him of another time. *I'll have to tell Brett about this.* Seeing Tony struggle to stand, Garret assisted him. His knees felt rubbery.

"Thanks."

"You're beat."

"Yeah. You guys get to carry the gear back to the chopper."

"No problem. You worked hard enough today. Let's go. This rain isn't letting up." Tony brought up the rear and fell behind. Garret made the others wait for him, though he insisted that he knew the way. "You took one for the team. We don't leave a man behind."

The acceptance felt good. Tony respected Garret and thought he had earned the same from the agent.

When they reached the helicopter, no one needed to say that it could not fly. Steady rain and clouds limited visibility. They climbed inside for shelter. Tony sighed.

"Since we're not going anywhere, I'm crawling in the back for a nap."

He shed his rain jacket and scrambled across the back seat. Finding several blankets, he appropriated one for a pillow, and offered the rest to his companions.

"Thanks," Garret said. "We'll call in our status and inventory this."

***

Tony woke when his stomach growled. He checked his watch. *Just past noon. Mom and Dad!* He sat up and groaned when he saw almost nothing. Heavy fog enshrouded the helicopter. Garret had been laying on the back seat.

"That's about how I feel. I got better things to do."

"My parents are coming this afternoon. They don't know about my son."

"You're just having a rotten week, aren't you."

"Character building. It's stopped raining. I can hike down before dark."

"Can we?"

"You seem to be in pretty good shape. I'll call Don and have him send someone with horses to meet us part way."

"Been years since I've been on a horse, but it's better than sitting here. Put on the headset and McKay will connect you. Tell him horses for two. Phillips will stay with the chopper."

"Anything to eat in here?"

Tony crawled across the seat and adjusted the headset. When McKay signaled him, he called Don.

"Reverend, what the heck you doing? Sleeping?"

Tony grinned.

"We're socked in. Garret and I are going to hike down. Can you send someone with horses to meet us?"

"Sure thing. I'll get Red right on it."

"Don, my parents will be there soon."

"Already here." Tony's heart sank. "Don't worry. I smoothed it over for you. They're talking to Kelly now."

"Thanks, Don."

"I'll put it on your tab. Now get moving."

Tony disconnected and pulled on his jacket. He grabbed an energy bar and canteen and climbed from the helicopter. Garret followed him with the evidence, back in the cargo netting. They moved as fast as the terrain and conditions allowed. The agent had no problem keeping up with Tony. In a half-hour they found themselves below the clouds. An hour later, they reached dry ground. The trail followed Elk Creek raging through a narrow canyon.

"Not a good place for a swim," Garret said.

"It's only this bad when the snow's melting or it rains."

"Most of the year."

"Yeah."

"How much of it looks like this?"

"About five miles, but this isn't the worst of it. Just wait."

They heard the worst of it before they could see it. The roar of the water made it impossible to talk without shouting. Huge boulders choked the canyon, forcing the water into an opening half the size of the rest of the channel. When Garret saw what lay beyond the boulders, his lips pursed in what must have been a whistle. The creek plummeted thirty feet into a bowl carved in the rock before continuing its mad plunge down the canyon. Garret held his comments until the trail took them away from the noise.

"I'd never heard of this park. I'll have to bring my kid here. He'll love it."

"I fell in love with this place my first day of work. I miss it every time I leave. I hate to think of not coming back."

"Don said you're a summer employee."

"Yeah. And I graduate seminary next spring."

"Don't take this wrong, Tony. You're a nice guy. You don't swear and you don't hold a grudge. But I can't imagine you as a minister."

"Sometimes I can't either."

They continued in silence. The trail leveled out with more soil and less rock.

"Do I hear bells?"

Tony laughed.

"Sleigh bells on the horses to let bears know they're coming."

"Why?"

"A lot of times bears avoid humans if they can. If you don't make any noise, you're more likely to surprise them."

"We haven't made much noise for the past couple hours."

"I know. I'm tired. Not thinking."

"Doesn't matter since we didn't see any bears."

Tony waved.

"Hi, Red!"

"Why's he called Red? His hair's black."

"His last name's Herring."

It took a moment for Garret to laugh.

"Someone has a dry sense of humor."

"Don."

"Figures."

***

Another agent picked up Garret and his evidence at the ranger station while Tony and Red unsaddled horses.

"Hello, son."

Tony wheeled and, with relief, saw his father's smiling face. They hugged.

"Good to see you, Dad."

"Yeah. You've had quite a week."

"Everybody keeps reminding me of that. All kinds of new experiences. Where's Mom?"

"I took her to Kelly's. They're cooking supper. He looks just like you did at that age."

"I know. You're okay with this?"

"Don't have much choice. But Don sat us down and gave us the lay of the land. He reminded us that you were both kids at the time and you both learned from your mistakes. He said Kelly's a nice girl and a great mother, said Brett's real well-behaved. I didn't get to spend much time with him yet, but Don was right. Kelly was nervous about meeting us. Made me like her because she feels guilty. Couldn't handle it if she thought what she did was okay. She said that she seduced you."

"She can't take all the responsibility. I had choices."

"That's right. But you were both nineteen. Kids sow wild oats. You turned out okay."

"Dad. I . . . may not finish school."

His father did not reply, but helped Tony put the horses in their stalls.

"Son, a lot of things have changed for you this past week. Maybe enough to make you rethink your future. We'll support whatever decision you make, as long as you ask the Lord's help and take your time making it."

"Thanks, Dad."

"You done here?"

"Yeah. I think I even have tomorrow off."

"Don said he's working the weekend so you and Kelly can have it off. Awful nice of him."

"Yeah. Guess he figures we've had a rough week too."

"So, how you like working with the FBI?"

"Pretty interesting. Those classes I took came in handy."

***

Tony's parents stayed overnight with him. He woke to the smell of bacon. *Mom's cooking.* When he rolled out of bed, every muscle protested. He shuffled to the kitchen.

"Morning, Tony," Amanda Wagner said. "You look like you're ninety."

"Feel like it too. I haven't climbed in ten months and that was a tough one."

"Sit. I'm making pancakes."

"Where's Dad?"

"He walked over to get Brett. Kelly's washing clothes this morning. She'll come when she's done."

"I need to do that too."

"Oh, I've already started."

"*Mom*, you're not my housekeeper."

"Just hush. I don't get many chances to take care of my kids anymore."

"That's because we're adults."

"I enjoy it. Now, about Kelly. She may be in love with you."

He choked on his coffee. After a few seconds, he decided to be blunt.

"It's just physical."

Her eyes widened.

"Um. I think there's more to it than that."

"You're right. She wants Brett to have his father around."

Amanda turned pancakes.

"I'm just saying there could be a future with her. You need to keep an open mind."

"When I open my mind I think about going to bed with her."

She dropped her spatula and turned to him slack-jawed.

"Where did this nerve come from all of a sudden? You've never been so outspoken."

"I don't have any more secrets, Mom. I'm just reminding you that I'm not perfect."

"I raised you. I know that. But honesty is good. You're a healthy, young man. Get married and you can have all the sex you want."

He choked again, then grinned.

"I've started something with my honesty. I understand I don't need to get married to get all I want."

"Don't you dare! I'll come out here and smack you around!"

Tony chuckled.

"Yes, ma'am. I'm confused right now, but I know enough to think through my actions to the consequences. Right away, I wanted to ask Kelly to marry me. Make things right. But I know that marriage needs serious consideration. I can't ask unless I'm sure that we share enough of the same values to make it work. I know how tough it is."

She set a plate in front of him and kissed his forehead.

"You've always had a lot of common sense."

"Almost always. There's my boy."

"Hi, Daddy. Grandpa walked with me."

"Good. I don't want you to come over here by yourself."

"Yes, sir." Tony pushed his chair back and lifted Brett to his lap with a groan. "What's wrong, Daddy?"

"I worked too hard yesterday. My muscles hurt."

Brett hugged him.

"I'm sorry."

"Thanks, son."

"Eat your pancakes," Amanda said. "Brett, would you like some of Grandma's blueberry pancakes?"

"Yes, ma'am."

"Come sit here so your daddy can eat."

***

When Kelly saw Tony's condition, she offered him a massage. She smiled when he hesitated.

"Your parents are here. I can't rape you."

He blushed.

"Okay." She worked on his shoulders, upper arms, and upper back, finding numerous knots. "You're pretty good at that."

"It's a family tradition. We all learned how to do it."

"Just don't do it when we're alone. And it's not you I don't trust." This time Kelly blushed, though only Amanda saw it. "That was a good start. I think I'll add a hot shower. You can keep Mom company."

"Go for it."

After he left, Amanda spoke.

"You like him, don't you."

Kelly barely hesitated.

"What's not to like?"

"You know what I mean."

"Yes. I know. I want Brett to have both his parents. That causes poor judgement. I want to love Tony, for Brett. And he's a great guy. If he was rotten, I'd see more clearly."

"He *is* a great guy, though I'm obviously not impartial. I'm playing matchmaker, I guess."

"Oh, my mother does the same thing. I always resisted. Because I hoped I'd find Tony. The little time we spent together impressed me so much. He has a conscience. He has character. He saved my life. I think I've had a crush on him ever since."

"Then you need to keep reminding yourself that he has faults. He's no knight in shining armor. He's just a regular guy with a lot of doubts."

"Thanks, Amanda. I'm afraid I've thought of him as my knight."

"Take the summer to get to know him, as a friend. By September, you'll know how you feel."

***

Tony typed "national park killer" and hit the search button on his computer. No complete matches. He changed the entry to "national park murders" and found links to numerous articles about murders in national parks. He scanned each, looking for the serial killer's MO. He printed those that matched, going back year after year. Ten in seven years. For a two-year period, he found nothing. He had almost given up when he discovered another, then another.

He examined his printouts, highlighting similarities. All victims were wealthy, lone hikers, robbed in one location, wounded there, then hunted down and killed. *Nothing I didn't know.* The killer struck in parks all over the western half of the country, although the two oldest were on the east coast. *Why the two year gap? Probably in jail for some unrelated offense. Or killing people somewhere besides national parks.*

Back at his computer, Tony changed his search criteria. "Robbery, murder, multiple gunshots, rural" produced hundreds of results. He painstakingly scanned the stories, thankful for the high-speed internet access. After more than an hour, his search yielded another match. A hiker in the Missouri Ozarks, during the two missing years. He felt elated, wondering how many more the FBI knew of. He continued searching, promising to stop when he found one more match. That required another hour. This one fell in the time frame of the first four murders. The location, western Tennessee.

"You worked your way west."

He stood, stretched and could not contain his curiosity. He needed to know how thorough his research had been. He called Garret at the lodge housing the FBI agents.

"Garret."

"Wow. I didn't really expect to get you. This is Tony."

"You think of something else?"

"No. I just have a stupid question."

"I have time for one stupid question."

"I've been researching this killer on the internet and wondered if I did a good job. Did you find more than fourteen victims?"

"Fourteen?"

"Yeah. That's all I could find, but I only spent about five hours on it."

"Fourteen?"

"Yeah."

"Did you print out anything on them?"

"Yeah."

"Bring it over."

"Now?"

"Yeah. We have ten."

"I must have messed up."

"Maybe. But I want to see it anyhow."

"Okay. Be there in fifteen minutes."

Tony pulled on a sweatshirt, gathered his papers and walked into the cool evening air. He considered his research criteria. They had seemed sound. *But I'd have to be pretty egotistical to think I could do a better job of research than the FBI.*

Garret waited at the door to his motel room. He held out his hand and Tony gave him the papers.

"Come in and close the door." Garret took a chair by the table and

Tony chose another. He waited in silence while the agent scanned each case, separating them into two piles. He scrutinized one pile a second time. "Hellfire!"

"I can't be right?"

"The hell you can't. I don't see anything wrong with your research. Serial killers tend to escalate, killing more often or becoming more violent as time passes. Whoever did our research got to that two year gap and figured they'd found the beginning. They also failed to consider that the killer may have operated outside of national parks. This is big, Tony."

Tony shrugged.

"I was just curious."

"You'd make a good investigator."

"Thanks. How does this help?"

"Four more cases means four more chances to find the clue that could catch this guy. Somewhere along the line, he's made mistakes. Enough mistakes leads us to him."

"The first four murders were on the east coast, then two in Tennessee and Missouri, the rest in the western half of the country. Does that mean he's moved?"

"Maybe. But we believe he travels. He may have just switched territory. This one probably doesn't hunt close to home. We believe he chooses national parks because no one will notice a car with out of state plates. We think he fancies himself a great outdoors man. He likes the challenge of stalking his victims, then getting out without being seen."

"He likes killing them slowly, doesn't he?"

"Yeah. Never less than four wounds. Only one is lethal. Real sick."

"You said he doesn't live around here. But he must have stuck around long enough to frame me."

"The place is full of tourists. He'd feel safe hanging around to watch the aftermath. He probably does it all the time. Not uncommon. He either chose you because you found the body or he saw you with the victim. He's done it before."

"What!"

"Only once. I didn't hear about it until today. That guy didn't have an airtight alibi. He spent weeks in jail. The unsub probably uses that method to dispose of the rifle after a few killings. Buys another one from a private owner. Gets a big laugh while we waste our time."

"I guess a sick sense of humor goes with a sick mind."

"Hand in hand. Though I know a lot of people with a sick sense of humor who aren't serial killers."

***

"I hear the FBI left town this morning," Don said over lunch at park headquarters.

"Don't know if that's good or not," Kevin commented. "They were a pain, but people felt safe with them here."

Tony washed down his sandwich before replying.

"The national park killer has never struck twice in the same place. There's no need for anybody to worry. And the only people who needed to worry in the first place were the macho, 'I don't need a hiking partner' types."

Don nodded.

"Tony's right. Glad Garret got that word out to the national media. Maybe people will think twice about hiking alone. They don't seem to listen to us."

"The macho types don't think they need to listen to anybody," Kelly said. "Tony, want to help me feed the cubs?"

"Yeah. Then we'd better get over to the trail head for our nature walk."

They filled bottles and left through the back door. Kevin shook his head.

"They act like parents."

"They are parents. But they feel responsible for the cubs."

"If Tony were any other guy, he'd have got naked with her by now. Anybody can see that she's hot for him. I'd tell him to get her to bed if I thought it'd do any good."

"What do you expect of the reverend? You know he's preaching at his church this Sunday?"

"Really? Too bad I have to work. That'd be worth seeing."

"I plan to sit in the front row and make faces at him."

Kevin laughed.

"That's about the only thing that gets you into a church."

"Oh, no. I go for weddings, funerals, and potlucks too."

"Be careful. People will think you're a holy roller."

Don laughed and walked out the back door.

"You two behaving yourselves?"

Tony snorted.

"What do you think?"

"Yes," Kelly said. "Unfortunately."

Tony blushed, but had a retort.

"You heard it, Don. Sexual harassment."

"Well, I believe you fight fire with fire."

The crimson deepened. Don laughed and disappeared inside. Kelly glanced at Tony, then turned her eyes to the ravenous cubs.

"I wouldn't mind."

Tony shifted the bottle to his left hand and surprised her by stroking her hair. He leaned close enough for her to feel his breath on her neck. When nothing more happened, she turned her head. He had three choices: kiss her, stay awkwardly close, or move away. He chose the former, conservatively. She smiled and caressed his cheek.

"I liked that."

"Me too."

"Maybe we could continue that off-duty."

"Don't tempt me."

"We can continue without ending up in bed. You have to start trusting yourself some time or you'll end up old and alone." He sighed, but kissed her again, this time liberally. When he finished, her cheeks had reddened. "Um-m. You're even better at that than I remembered. But I've taken some precautions to keep you out of my bed."

"What kind of precautions?"

"No contraceptives. And I sleep with both bedroom doors open. Brett would be very upset if he discovered my door closed."

"Pretty smart."

"So come over tonight. Don't be afraid."

"I am coming over. Remember, it's your turn to cook?"

"I'm ordering pizza. But stay after Brett goes to bed tonight."

"I'll think about it."

***

What am I doing? Tony resisted the urge to turn and run as he walked up Kelly's sidewalk. He had needed a cold shower just thinking about this evening. He made it to the door and hugged Brett, but his eyes found her. While they waited for the pizza, he wrestled with his son, hoping to wear him out so he would go to bed early.

Kelly paid the pizza deliveryman and sent Brett to wash for supper. Tony wrapped his arms around her and they shared a very intense kiss. When he moved his lips to her neck, she stifled a shriek. They did not notice Brett until he hugged both of them. Tony jerked away, then picked up his son.

"When I saw you hugging Mommy, I wanted to hug you too."

"Well, thanks. Let's eat."

Tony had no idea what flavor pizza he ate. His mind bounced between being unaware of anything but Kelly, and reproaching himself for his frame of mind. She tried not to flirt with him, keeping her eyes on Brett and her food.

After supper, Tony wrestled with his son until Kelly told him to stop or Brett would be too excited to sleep. Tony chose a book from Brett's collection, Bible stories, and began reading to him. The subject helped adjust his frame of mind. When she told Brett to get ready for bed, he left her alone, going to the refrigerator for ice water instead.

He gave his son a hug and kiss goodnight, then waited for Kelly on the sofa. When she returned, she did not immediately join him.

"How are you?"

"Not so out of control."

"Good. I really don't want to go to bed with you."

"Okay. Will you marry me?"

She sank into the nearest chair. A long silence followed.

"I'd marry you, if I thought you were asking for the right reason. But I want to marry for love, not because you feel responsible for me and our son."

He bit his lip.

"Are you saying that you love me?"

"I think so."

He ran his hands through his hair.

"You're right about one thing. I'm asking for the wrong reason. But you're wrong about it being a noble reason. I want you so bad I can hardly stand myself. I want to marry you so I can get you in bed."

"Oh. That's honesty. Maybe you'd like to go."

"But you're not asking me to leave."

"No. You won't force yourself on me. You just may end up miserable if you stay."

"That's my problem."

She advanced as if in slow motion. When she reached him, he pulled her into his lap for a very long kiss. His hand crept close to her breasts, but he pulled back. He stroked her neck instead and felt her shudder. She pushed away a little and unbuttoned his shirt with trembling hands. When he kissed her neck, she slid her hand inside. He groaned and nearly shoved her on the floor.

Kelly sat beside him as he doubled over, hiding his face in his arms.

"I'm sorry," she said.

"For what? I just have a low tolerance for female attention."

She rubbed his back.

"I'm sorry I started this."

"I have choices. I could have stopped any time. Would you marry me if I promised to love you?"

"Oh, Tony. You sound like a seminary student trying to get laid."

His shoulders shook until his laugh became audible. He sat up, grinning at her.

"That's what I am. I could be falling in love with you, but my body's making it hard to think. Don't you want to get married so I can think straight?"

"And if you discover that you don't love me?"

"You'd never know it. I'll pretend to love you until I do."

Kelly wiped tears away.

"That's so sweet. I really think you should wait until your brain tells you to ask again. I don't trust decisions that originate in your jeans."

He sighed.

"Why do you have to be so sensible? What happened to the girl who jumped my bones the day we met?"

"She got pregnant."

"Good point. I can't talk you into this?"

"No. Not tonight."

"Okay. I'd better go. I've tortured myself long enough."

***

With the minister gone for a Sunday, most churches saw a dramatic drop in attendance. But news of the substitute had spread throughout Spruce Lake. People who did not belong to the church packed the pews. Tony peeked out at the crowd and took a deep breath. *No need to feel nervous.* Just follow the format, like reading a script. Pastor Johnson had written the sermon for him. He had nearly memorized it, but had also marked the text to make it easier if he lost his train of thought.

Don't look at Don. Keep your eyes on the back of the church, right over everyone's head. You've done this a dozen times, in front of your professors. No one here is grading you. Right! If you stutter through this, you'll never hear the end of it.

This suit is hot. How does the pastor do it every Sunday? He wears a short sleeved shirt under his robe. That's loose. Probably cooler than this suit.

Don't be nervous. Be grateful. Look at the opportunity the Lord has put in front of you. Some of these people never set foot in church. He'll help you deliver the message. Tony smiled. He had all the help he needed to get through this service.

He followed the script: Hymn, liturgy, gospel reading, hymn, sermon. *Just like you practiced. Made it! All downhill from here.* Hymn, offering, prayer of thanks for members with a new baby, blessing, final hymn, announcements. Tony left the church without tripping over his feet and waited by the door to shake hands with worshipers.

Don came out grinning.

"You didn't stumble once, reverend. I'm disappointed. I was hoping for a good laugh."

His wife, Lois, hit him.

"You did a wonderful job, Tony. Why don't you come for dinner?"

"Sorry, Lois, I have a standing date with Brett."

"Oh, we've invited them too."

"Okay. We'll be there as soon as I'm done here."

Tony greeted and accepted compliments from others, including Betty. She hugged him.

"You did great."

"Thanks, Betty."

Brett grinned and shook his hand.

"Daddy, you preach as good as the pastor."

"Thanks, son." He grinned at Kelly. "I hear you get out of cooking."

"We'll eat better, I'm sure. All the baked stuff Don's brought has been great."

"Lois is a great cook. I'll be out in a few minutes."

After greeting the last parishioner, Tony joined Kelly and Brett on the playground and they walked to Don's house adjacent to the ranger station. Kelly inhaled.

"Smells good in here. Your cooking must be as good as your baking. Can I help with anything?"

"There's a couple salads in the fridge," Lois said. "You boys go relax on the deck until we call you."

"First step to relaxing is getting out of this coat and tie," Tony said.

He hung them on a hook and followed Don outside while unbuttoning his collar. Brett immediately saw the slide.

"Can I play on it, Daddy?"

"If it's okay with Don."

"That's what it's there for."

"Just don't get dirty."

They sat and watched Brett play for a while.

"He's a cute kid," Don said.

"Thanks. Smart and well-behaved too. Kelly's done a great job with him."

"You're doing a great job too. Why don't you ask her to marry you?"

"I did. She turned me down."

"Hard to believe."

"She won't marry me unless I love her."

"Of course you love her."

"How would you know? I don't even know."

"You don't? It's plain as the nose on your face."

"Not to me. I know that I'd like to get her in bed. But love? That's hard to tell."

"You look like a man in love, not in lust. Other people see it too. You just aren't thinking straight."

"You said it. You really think I love her?"

"You bet. I've known you six years now. You've never acted like this around a woman. And I've seen you in lust. Remember Elly?"

Tony blushed.

"She knew how to tease. Thank God she hooked up with somebody else. Maybe I'll ask Kelly again. All she can do is say no."

"Good. Now, I think it's time you decided about your future. Kevin's leaving."

"Why?"

"Four kids are too much. He's taking a job with his father-in-law so her folks can help them out. He won't leave me high and dry. He's staying till after Labor Day, but he's moving her and the kids next weekend. I'll put in a good word for you if you apply for his position."

Tony studied his hands.

"Wow. Law enforcement. You know how much I'd like that."

Don grinned.

"I'm counting on it."

"I'll think about it. Just don't tell Kelly."

"I'm posting the job tomorrow morning."

"Let her find out then. I need a few hours to think about it–pray about it--before I discuss it."

"Okay. Guess I'd expect that of you. Kevin's house will be available. Nice place for a family starting out."

"Yes, Don."

***

Tony seldom prayed on his knees, but he did that night. Then he let go of the decision. He woke in the morning with his answer. Apply for the job. *If I get it, God's telling me to leave the seminary.* He reached the ranger station ahead of schedule. When he asked for an application, Don grinned.

"I'll write my recommendation and attach it before I send it in."

"Thanks."

Tony completed the paperwork and returned it to Don before Kelly arrived. She glanced at the bulletin board while drinking her first cup of coffee. Tony saw her stop in mid-sip, then put her finger on the job listing. She faced him.

"Did you see this?"

"I already applied for it."

Her smile made his heart race. Then she noticed Don watching them.

"Brett would love that."

"That's what I was thinking," Tony agreed.

"You two are so full of it," Don said. "Someone should lock you in a room for about a week."

They both blushed.

"Just mind your own business, Don."

"Oh, get to work. Tired of listening to you."

Kelly hugged Tony.

"I want you to stay. But I wanted it to be your decision. I wouldn't ask you."

"I appreciate that. Even with no outside influence, it was tough trying to figure out what the Lord wanted me to do."

"But you've decided He wants you to leave the seminary?"

"No-o. I'll know when I find out about this job."

"Aren't you a shoo in? Don will recommend you."

"It'll really help. But other rangers with more seniority might want to transfer here. Seniority is everything."

"I got a job here. I didn't have a lot of seniority."

"Thanks for the encouragement."

"Don't mention it. What time do you plan to come for supper tonight?"

"What time do you want me?"

"Doesn't matter. My landlord's gone and I promised to water their lawn. I'll have to move the sprinklers a few times, so I need to get started before I work on supper."

"I'll change, then come help you move sprinklers."

"You don't have to do that."

"How about if I do it this way? I'll wear my swimsuit so Brett and I can play in the sprinklers while I'm moving them around."

"Oh, he'll love that. Under those conditions, I accept your help."

***

Kelly sat on the back porch watching them, or rather, Tony, play in the water. The difference between his build now and the body he had at nineteen astonished her. She remembered a nice physique, but still boyish and smooth.

Now he possessed muscles that made her temperature rise. In uniform, she had noticed his strong arms, but somehow it had never occurred to her that the rest of his body would match. Broad shoulders blended into a sizable chest that no one would call smooth. Though he did not have six-pack abs, she found them very acceptable. Her eyes traveled downward, reluctantly leaving his swim trunks for the muscle definition of his thighs and calves.

Who am I kidding when I tell him I don't want sex? I want that man in my bed! Oh, do I ever! He needs to be a ranger, because a minister shouldn't look that good.

"Mommy, come play with us!"

"I don't have my swim suit on. I have to check my supper pretty soon. I'll just watch you and your daddy."

"Come on, Mommy!"

"Yeah," Tony said. "Don't sit on the sidelines."

His smile sent tingling sensations all over her body.

"You two just quit worrying about me and play."

"What do you think, Brett? Should we get her out here?"

"Yeah!"

Tony leaped on the porch in one stride. *Like some pine forest Tarzan.* She flushed with anticipation, but protested.

"Don't you dare!"

He laughed as he scooped her up. Kelly giggled and slipped her arms around his neck. When he carried her into the sprinkler, she shrieked. Brett squealed.

"You're all wet, Mommy!"

"I noticed." She trailed her fingers down Tony's neck to that hard chest, the water providing excellent lubrication. She lowered her voice. "Now that you have me, what do you plan to do with me?"

Tony's smile faded, but he showed no inclination to release her. When he licked his lips, she groaned and kissed him.

Brett failed to notice his parents' embrace, having become fascinated with the water filling up his toy truck.

Kelly straightened her body and Tony let her slide through his hands until her feet reached the ground. He moved his hands up her sides until they caressed her breasts. All without their lips parting.

She felt light-headed. *If we were alone, I'd wrap my legs around you and do you right here. No birth control. Who cares! You make beautiful babies. Take me!*

But what to do with Brett?

Tony's fingers stirred and she dug hers into his shoulders. *How can this not effect him?* She soon had her answer, feeling more than his swim trunks.

He pushed away and turned toward the sprinkler. After a dazed moment, Kelly walked back to the porch, squeezing the water from her shirt. *I knew it wasn't going to happen. Why am I so disappointed?*

She changed to dry clothes, checked her supper, and brought towels to the porch. Tony still played with Brett, but with less animation and a subdued smile. He moved the sprinklers, then joined her. She handed him a towel which he used on his hair before speaking.

"I'm sorry. That was my fault."

She nodded.

"I guess you could say that. Although you didn't do it intentionally."

"I wasn't thinking."

"Well, you weren't thoughtless. You were just naive. It didn't occur to you how horny I'd get seeing you in swim trunks."

He pulled on his t-shirt to hide a smile.

"I took it way too far. I shouldn't have touched you like that."

"Oh, but I liked it."

"So I noticed. But I crossed the line. That's no way to stay out of bed."

"Definitely not. Is that your goal with women, to stay out of bed?"

"Since a little flood in Wisconsin. Even before that, I never started anything. I may have been thinking about sex, but I never made the first move."

"It wasn't just me?"

"No. I've always been that way. And I always made the lame attempt to talk her out of it."

"I remember. How'd you overcome that and learn to refuse?"

"I didn't. I quit dating."

"That's pretty extreme."

"I scared myself. My first year of seminary, I dated a conservative girl from my college, and I nearly went too far. And too far with her was less than what we just did. She'd barely been kissed. I lay awake all night thinking about sex and nearly flunked a test the next day. I told myself I quit dating because I needed the time to study. But I was scared of what I'd do."

"You must've matured out of that. You stopped last time and again today."

"Maybe I have. Finally. It's only been a couple years since I had a close call."

"Oh?"

"Yeah." She rested her chin on her hand and stared at him. "You want to hear about that?"

"All the juicy details."

He smiled.

"Why?"

"Why not?"

"She was a summer worker and she came looking for conquests. If she hadn't picked me first, I wouldn't have been so attracted to her. She slept with a lot of men before the summer was over. I tried to avoid being alone with her. She came over to my apartment and I wouldn't go inside. I wouldn't even follow her. Gil and Betty got quite a kick out of that. 'Why are you standing out there, Tony? Elly's in my apartment.' I even fell asleep on their deck once."

"Persistent woman."

"Didn't really understand the concept of 'no' either. She gave up trying to seduce me off duty and cornered me in the stable. I made that lame attempt to discourage her, but she ignored it."

"Like I did."

"No. I never felt the same kind of pressure with you. I didn't make the second move with her. Or the third or fourth. She was getting my pants off and hers. The only move I would have made was the final one. I just surrendered, like that would absolve me of blame. I had feet and I'm a lot stronger than she was. I could have pushed her away, like I just did with you."

"You nearly shoved me on the floor last time. So what stopped you?"

"Don. He listened before he busted in on us. He told her if he caught her fooling around on company time again, he'd fire her. She got indignant, wondered why he hadn't threatened me. Then he really lit into her. She never bothered me again."

"Your guardian angel."

They both laughed.

"You call him that. See what he says."

***

Tony answered the phone.

"Evergreen National Park."

"Tony," Agent Garret said. "I need your help. Will your boss loan you out?"

"You can ask him."

"Want to take a road trip?"

"Ah-h. I like working with you. Will this jeopardize my job?"

"Not a chance. The park service has promised complete cooperation. You'll get your usual salary, the Bureau will just reimburse the Park Service for your time."

"Okay. I'll let you talk to Don."

He yelled at Don to pick up the phone, then disconnected. Kelly squinted.

"Was that the FBI?"

"Yeah. Garret wants my help again."

"Here?"

"No. He said a road trip."

"How long?"

"I don't know. He wouldn't want me unless there's been another killing, would he?"

"I'd think your expertise would only be needed for a new crime scene. But there must be rangers in another park who could do what you can."

"Remember, Garret doesn't trust people."

"True."

"Tony," Don said. "Go home and pack for a few days. And wear civies. Garret doesn't want anyone to know you're a ranger. Someone will pick you up at your place in about an hour."

"Did he say anything else?"

"Just that there's been another murder. The SOB is escalating, just like they said he would. It's less than two months since he killed here. Be careful."

"I always am. And I'll be with the FBI. How much safer can I be?"

Kelly walked outside with him.

"I'll miss you."

"I'll miss you too. I'll stop and say good bye to Brett before I go home."

"He'll appreciate that."

He caressed her cheek, then kissed her.

"I'll be home soon."

"Take care of yourself."

***

Tony visited with Gil and Betty until a Federal car pulled into the driveway. The FBI agent took him to the nearest airport, twenty miles from Spruce Lake. They waited by the facility's only three hangars for twenty minutes before a sleek, small jet landed.

"There's your ride," the agent said, the longest sentence he had uttered to Tony.

"Cool."

Tony grabbed his bag and waited while the jet taxied to them. The door opened before it completely stopped, and an agent waved him in. He had barely boarded, when the engines revved. The agent closed the door and took his bag.

"Welcome aboard, Tony. Have a seat," Garret said. "For those of you who don't know, this is Ranger Tony Wagner. You will refer to him as a consultant. No one in the park is to know that he's a ranger."

"Where this time?"

"Grand Teton. We may have more rock climbing for you. This time you'll be better equipped."

"Good. I hate to waste time."

Garret gave him an FBI jacket and a name badge reading, T. Wagner, FBI consultant.

"Here's the preliminary report. We have maps so you can familiarize yourself with the area we'll be going into."

"Topographic maps?"

"Yeah. Let us know if you find anything significant."

Tony read the report, then studied the maps. He took notes before reporting to Garret.

"The terrain is really similar to what we saw in Evergreen. Rugged, canyons, looks like trees. It's very isolated, the only trail within miles."

"That's his MO. People, I want pictures of the tourists. There's a good chance that our killer has stayed around to enjoy the show."

After examining the map further, Tony tried to doze, but had to admit that he was far too excited to sleep. He pretended to study the map while observing people. Most of them slept, having learned everything they could before reaching the crime scene. Garret made frequent phone calls. Another agent worked on a computer.

The short flight ended at the Jackson Hole Airport. Two government SUVs waited there. Garret pointed Tony to the same vehicle he rode in.

Tony took in the scenery as they drove north on Highway 26, then west on Teton Park Road. The SUVs followed the signs directing visitors to the town of Moose and park headquarters. A half-mile off the Teton Park Road, they pulled into the parking lot.

The ranger-in-charge met them just inside.

"Gentlemen, I'm Tom Sloan."

"Ranger Sloan, I'm Agent Garret." He introduced the rest of his team, calling Tony his back country expert. "Let's get started."

Sloan led them to a conference room and walked to a large wall map of the park.

"We found Mr. Weller here, in Cascade Canyon, on the Lake Solitude Trail. It's classified a strenuous day hike. Eighteen point four miles, 2252 foot elevation change, should take ten hours." He sounded like a park service brochure. "Some hikers like to take it in two days. Weller got an overnight camping permit."

"What do we know about Mr. Weller?"

"He's local, from Jackson. Successful businessman. Wife. Three kids."

"Do we have the autopsy report?"

"Preliminary." Sloan shuffled through papers and handed one to Garret. "Shot in both legs and his right arm. The kill shot was to the back of the head. It was messy."

"Crime scene photos?"

Sloan gave him an envelope.

"Everything that we have is here on this table."

"Thank you, Ranger Sloan. We won't need you until we've had a chance to study this." Sloan left, closing the door behind him, while Garret handed out assignments. "Tony, see if that map shows you anything ours didn't. The chopper will take us there in 45 minutes."

***

Tony relaxed and enjoyed the helicopter flight. The sun brought out the contrast between the ice fields and the dark granite of the mountains. The pilot hovered over the taped off crime scene before proceeding to his landing site almost three-quarters of a mile away.

"Tony," Garret said. "It's too late in the day to bother with your climbing gear. Help us with the other stuff. We'll camp by the helicopter tonight."

Tony nodded and led the team up the trail. Garret survey the area outside the tape and directed everyone to a badly disturbed area.

"No one outside this perimeter unless you're investigating or heading back down the trail."

He compared photos to the terrain, discussing trajectory with one of the other team members.

Tony stayed out of the way until someone needed him. He walked to the tape and studied the area inside it's boundaries, about thirty by a hundred feet. A large, dark stain lay twenty feet from him. Smaller stains lay beyond that. He wanted a closer look, but obeyed orders instead.

"Tony, follow me."

He ducked under the tape after Garret, observing while awaiting further orders. The blood trail seemed smeared, as if the victim had dragged himself toward cover. That fit. It began with a large stain, perhaps sixty feet from where the body was found.

Tony continued on the back trail, searching for the directional spatter left by a wounded man, running for his life. He reached the tape, then retraced his steps, certain that he had missed the drops of blood.

"What are you scowling at?"

Tony looked up.

"Nothing."

"When I ask for your opinion, I want to hear it."

"Where's the blood trail? There's a lot about crime scene investigation that I don't know, but I can follow a blood trail."

"It starts over there."

Garret pointed to the first large stain.

"The one in Evergreen covered more than a mile."

"So why's this one so short? Think about it. I'll ask for your theories later. But right now, I want you to look up there." He pointed to a slope sprinkled with boulders and spruce. "That's our best guess where the initial shot came from. If you find anything, place a marker."

Tony retrieved markers, glad to feel useful. He crisscrossed the slope, climbing on top of every rock big enough to hold a sniper. He hoped that the body recovery team had obeyed the orders in the FBI bulletin. "Tape off the scene. Photograph the scene and body. Remove the body and associated evidence. Leave." Garret wanted no amateurs disturbing his crime scene.

The oblong impression leaped out at him. About six inches long, and no more than two at it's widest point. The depression left by a rifle butt. Too deep for a rifle leaning against a tree. Someone had used it to lever himself to his feet. He placed a marker, then crouched to survey the needle-covered ground under the Spruce tree.

Two scuff marks lay about six feet beyond the impression. Someone had laid on his belly here, waiting. He began trembling. *Calm down, Tony. This doesn't make you a brilliant detective.* He followed his own advice before backing away and calling to Garret.

He and another agent hurried up the slope.

"What you got?"

"Looks like the spot where the shooter waited."

Garret studied the impression and the ground around it.

"Good job." He turned to the other agent. "Get pictures, casts, and every pine needle under this tree. If he dropped an eyelash, I want it collected. Tony, keep looking. Check his most likely routes to this spot."

An hour passed. Tony worked his way down the canyon for fifty yards, then returned to the site and back the other way. Thirty yards west, he almost missed it, off to his left, nearly invisible at that angle. He placed another marker.

"Garret!"

Tony thought he saw a smile flicker across the senior agent's face as he closed the distance. Garret crouched beside the marker.

"Is that what I think it is?"

"Do you think it's a mocassin print?"

"Yeah."

"Haven't seen many of those, but that's what I think it is. I don't see any others, so there's no way of knowing how big the guy is."

"We'll get that from the body impression. This will give us his shoe size and weight. It's a whole lot more than we had. I think you missed your calling."

Tony felt his heart pounding against his chest and tried not to smile.

"You said he was bound to make a mistake sooner or later. I'll keep looking."

"Don't sell yourself short. You have the potential to be a good investigator."

When Tony turned away, he quit fighting the smile. Garret did not throw praise around. Tony had yet to hear him say anything more than "Good job" to anyone else. No job had ever given him quite the thrill he felt today. He had only come close to that feeling the last time he had worked with the FBI.

Maybe Garret's right. Maybe I missed my calling. But he saw no point in pursuing those thoughts. He had a family now. He needed to settle into one of the two careers in which he already had training.

***

Garret called off the search as darkness approached. They hiked back to the helicopter, where the pilot had set up camp. After stowing evidence and equipment in the aircraft, most of the agents poured coffee and sank into camp chairs.

Tony put enough distance between him and the other men to muffle their voices, sitting with his back against a boulder. He nearly dozed off before he heard footsteps approaching. Garret handed him a plate.

"Hope you like MREs."

"They fill the void. Thanks. I lost track of time."

Garret settled on a log.

"Stay out here and you're liable to end up bear food."

Tony nodded toward the other men.

"Not with the noise they're making. I've just had enough people for one day. I needed some alone time."

"And you want to be a minister?"

"Good point. I've applied for a full-time job with the park service."

"No kidding? Same thing you're doing now?"

"Law enforcement. I'd get to carry a gun again. I miss my gun."

Garret grinned.

"I understand. And you wouldn't have to leave your kid."

"Yeah."

"Or his mother."

"Yeah. Don't know quite what to do about that."

"You have time. So give me your thoughts on the size of the crime scene."

"In Evergreen, he wounded the guy in the arm first. He could still run. This guy must have been hit in the leg first. All he could do was try to crawl away."

"That explains the size. What about the motivation?"

"If this guy enjoys the thrill of the hunt, where's the sport in shooting your prey in the leg? The news stories don't give those details. What were the other crime scenes like?"

"Evergreen."

"Oh." Tony finished his food. "Could there have been other hikers in the area? Maybe he couldn't take the chance of hunting like he wanted to."

"That's a possible explanation. The profilers call him an organized serial killer. He doesn't like to deviate from his routine. However, the urge to kill may have been strong enough to force him to change. We'll have to see where the evidence leads. You ready to be sociable again?"

"Yeah. Am I coming across as anti-social?"

"No. You're coming across as a guy who doesn't feel like he fits in."

"I don't."

"Stick with me. You up to looking at crime scene photos on a full stomach?"

"I saw a guy after a bear had lunched on him."

"How could I forget? You handled that well enough to convince me you were a cold-blooded killer."

Tony shrugged.

"It bothers me. But I guess I handle it with faith. Death is part of life."

"Now you sound like a seminary student."

Garret selected chairs and handed him the pictures. Tony examined them by lantern light. Reaching the third, he dropped it to his lap and looked at the stars, swallowing several times. Garret grinned.

"The head shot?"

"Yeah."

"You really can handle this stuff. I've seen rookies lose their lunch over less than that."

"M-m. He must have upgraded his caliber when he bought the new gun."

"You're right. That damage was caused by a 30.06, not a .222."

"Looks like a cannon." He retrieved the pictures. "Were you hoping to make me lose my lunch?"

"No." Garret nodded toward the other agents. "You disappointed some of them. I'm hoping to figure out how good you really are. You're better than your training."

Tony felt like a school kid when the teacher praised his work. He shrugged again.

"I've always been curious. And I guess I notice a lot of things most people miss."

"That makes you one of us, Tony."

***

The next day, they searched for Weller's blaze orange backpack. Garret agreed with Tony's assertion that Cascade Creek seemed the most convenient disposal sight. He sent Phillips and Egan looking along the canyon wall, while everyone else concentrated on the often challenging terrain beside the creek.

The painstaking process of scrutinizing every snag, boulder, and pool took them a mile past the helicopter by noon. Garret sank to a log and opened an energy bar.

"I've never crawled over so many rocks in my life. We'll keep at this until three. If we don't find it by then, we'll have the rangers put out a bulletin offering a reward. It could be in Jenny Lake by now."

They pushed on after lunch. Tony had to admit that the strenuous work detracted from the rugged beauty of the canyon. The waterfalls and rapids which provided its name, lost their appeal. On the occasions when he had a view of the majestic Tetons, he barely looked up.

Even when he spotted the backpack, he felt less than elated. He called to Garret with no particular enthusiasm.

"I found it."

Garret passed the word along with greater animation.

"Over here!"

Tony sat on a rock, arms and legs crossed, when Garret reached him. The older man's grin faded.

Weller's backpack hung from a branch caught at the top of a waterfall. Though the creek only dropped about ten feet, the water boiled around boulders at its base.

Tony sighed and Garret slapped his back.

"Good job. I'll radio for your equipment. Anything else?"

"Blankets. We need to get above the fall."

He dragged himself to his feet while Garret called Phillips and Egan to return to the helicopter for Tony's equipment. He could not retrieve the backpack without venturing into the icy water. Snow melt. Probably cold enough to freeze if it stood still long enough.

When he reached a suitable spot above the waterfall, he removed his boots and socks, then replaced the boots. He shed his jacket and shirt when the equipment arrived. He answered Garret's unasked question.

"I want to have some dry clothes when I get done. I'd strip down to my underwear, but when I fall the jeans will protect me some."

"*When* you fall?"

"You ever tried walking in water moving that fast?"

"No."

"It's not a matter of 'if', it's 'how many times' it will knock me down. I'll tie the rope off here and try to work my way out to that boulder. If I can get the rope around that, I can go straight to the backpack. It will be your job to feed me line. Don't even think about asking me to put that thing in a sack before it gets to shore."

Garret grinned.

"Wouldn't want you to quit on me."

Tony secured the rope, checked his equipment, stepped into the creek, and immediately began shivering. When the water reached his knees, the current pulled his feet out from under him. The frigid water took his breath away. He struggled upright, gasping, bracing himself against the rope. He fought his way back upstream, this time making it above the boulder.

Water swirling around the rock had created a waist-deep pocket. He fell again coming out of it. Letting the rope hold him against the current, he worked his way to the edge of the waterfall. Here the creek did not reach his knees, but his feet threatened to slip on the treacherous rock. He examined his options and found only one sensible plan.

He dropped to his hands and knees, crawling toward the backpack. Garret continued to feed him line at just the right pace. Tony could not feel his hands or feet. The rest of his body had never felt so cold. His teeth chattered.

With one final effort, he grasped the shoulder strap, visually checking his numb fingers to be sure. He pulled himself away from the edge and felt the tug of the rope. He looped the strap over his arm for safekeeping before standing.

He leaned on the rope, letting the men on shore do most of the work. He stayed on his feet until he rounded the boulder, then fell twice more. The second time, they simply pulled him through the water. Garret jumped into the creek to drag him out.

The next few minutes passed in a fog for Tony. Someone helped him out of his clothes and wrapped him in blankets. Someone helped him drink coffee. People talked, but none of the words registered. Slowly, his head cleared and he became aware of the intense cold and uncontrollable shivering.

Garret crouched to eye level.

"You back with us?" Tony nodded. "I owe you another one. As soon as you can move, we'll get you to the chopper and back to a warm bed."

"G-g-good."

***

Tony barely remembered the rest of the day. He woke the next morning in a rustic motel room under a pile of blankets, one of them obviously electric. He did not bother to look around until he heard someone move. Garret poured coffee.

"How you feeling this morning?"

"Just warm enough. I didn't think you'd have to share a room."

"I don't. Someone had to keep an eye on you."

"Thanks." Tony dislodged the blankets and sat up, taking the coffee Garret offered. "I hate getting that cold."

"It's dangerous. The paramedic said you should see a doctor if you get sick from this. Could be pneumonia."

"I will."

Garret walked to the open door between their room and the next.

"When you get organized, come in here."

In ten minutes, Tony joined him in what turned out to be a conference room. The backpack and its contents covered the large table. Garret drank his coffee while Tony examined the individually bagged items. He hesitated, then his eyes met Garret's.

"Weller's watch and rings."

"Yeah."

"No one would carry that in their backpack. If I planned to take them off, I'd do it before I left on the hike."

"Seems reasonable."

"The killer took them and dumped everything?"

"So it would appear."

Tony ran his hand through his hair, leaving it standing on end.

"Why? He kept souvenirs of his other murders."

"You tell me."

Tony walked the length of the table without really seeing the evidence. He wandered to the window, noticed the rising sun shining on the Tetons, the reflection of the mountains on Jenny Lake. He faced Garret.

"Mistakes. Different caliber gun. No hunt. No robbery. A copycat?"

"A distinct possibility. I'll even say a probability. While we were in the mountains, Ferguson and Dimaggio were in Jackson, digging up everything they could on the victim. Your job is done. You could go home. Want to stick around?"

"Yes!"

Garret chuckled.

"You've earned the right. After breakfast, we'll see what we have."
***

The team sat around the cleared conference table, listening to Ferguson and Dimaggio report.

Weller had operated a successful ski and bike shop in Jackson for fifteen years. In the past five he had opened similar shops in two other resort areas.

Though active in civic affairs and a big contributor to community projects, he had few friends. Dimaggio flipped through his notebook.

"And I quote. 'Big shot. Pompous. Jerk.' To name a few. Of course, these terms were usually preceded by, 'I hate to speak ill of the dead.' The man had enemies."

"Anybody stand out?" Garret asked.

"His former business partner. They parted under less than agreeable terms. Former competition. Seems Weller played dirty. We're still checking into a rumor of an affair."

"Does the wife know about the rumor?"

"Couldn't get her away from the kids to ask. She admitted that they had their problems." He raised his fingers to form quotation marks. "Like all married couples. Other sources said the marriage was pretty rocky. Three different witnesses reported public screaming matches."

"You two keep digging into the possible affair. Egan, you and Phillips take the former business partner. Vasquez and Finch, the competition. Tony and I will revisit the widow Weller. And everybody circulate that sketch of Tony's hiker. We'll meet here again at 5:00. If Weller isn't a victim of our unsub, we need to prove it and move on."

Tony settled into the passenger seat of the Yukon and said nothing until Garret turned south on Highway 26.

"Can I ask you a question?"

"Shoot."

"I've never heard you address anyone but me by their first name."

The corner of Garret's mouth turned up.

"I'm waiting for the question."

"Why?"

"Using last names keeps some distance between us. Solidifies the chain of command. You're a volunteer. And a dedicated one. I need to treat you better than I do most people, or you'll tell me to go to hell."

Tony laughed.

"Well, that's honest. But I wouldn't use those words."

"No. You practice what you preach. Another thing. You won't say what you're really thinking if I act like an SOB."

"You figured that out?"

"That cold-blooded facade fooled me at first. I'm usually better at sizing up people. Nobody will bully you into anything. Browbeating will only hold you back."

"I've never let anyone push me into anything."

"So I'll try not to push. The Bureau offers some courses in Denver. When the Park Service hires you full-time, consider getting certified to investigate felonies."

"I haven't got the job yet."

"They're not stupid. Think about it."

"I will. Thanks." He sighed. "I know this is serious business, but I'm having the time of my life."

***

The big man who came to the door of the sprawling house on the outskirts of Jackson, introduced himself as Mrs. Weller's father. Both of her parents stayed with her when they gathered in the den for the interview. Wearing a sweat suit and no makeup, the widow Weller had dark circles under her puffy eyes.

Her father spoke first.

"Is this necessary? Two other agents asked her questions yesterday."

"I'm afraid so, Mr. Marvin," Garret said. "Your grandchildren were in the room yesterday. The agents couldn't ask all of the questions they needed to. And there have been some developments since then."

"You have a suspect?"

"We have leads. Mrs. Weller, I know this is a very difficult time for you. But I'm sure that you want to do everything you can to help catch your husband's killer."

"Of course."

"Did you know that your husband was having an affair?"

Marvin inhaled in advance of an outraged protest, but Garret silenced him with one of his uni-brow looks.

Tony barely took his eyes off the widow. She would probably make a lousy poker player. She thought about lying. Discarded the idea. Considered falling apart to avoid the question. Finally, she let her breath out.

"I suspected."

"Did you also suspect with whom he was having an affair?"

"Connie Armstrong."

"Local?"

"Yes."

"Married?"

"Yes."

"Husband's name?"

"Hunter."

"Did you share your suspicions with anyone?"

She sighed. Thought about it.

"Mom. My sister, June."

"Mrs. Marvin, did you pass that along?"

"She told me," the father said. "But what does this have to do with Jason's murder? I thought it was a serial killer."

"This does resemble the work of the National Park serial killer. But we wouldn't be doing our jobs if we ignored all other possibilities. We have agents pursuing other leads. Who did you tell, Mr. Marvin?"

"We all sat down as a family." His daughter looked shocked. "I'm sorry, honey. We tried to figure out how we could get proof for you to use in a divorce settlement."

"So Mrs. Weller wasn't at this family meeting. Who was?"

"My wife. Our other daughter. And our three sons."

"Names."

"June Rail. Everett, Peter, and Lawrence Marvin."

"Are any of those people here today?"

"Everett's out in the back yard with the kids. I'll tell you where to find the rest. They all live in the area."

"June will be back later this morning," Mrs. Weller said. "Do you think one of my family killed Jason?"

"As I said, ma'am, we're exploring all possibilities. Right now, I need to talk to them to find out how many people knew about this affair. If it got back to Mr. Armstrong, that would make him a viable suspect. We need to collect as much information as we can. For instance, Mr. Marvin, would you be willing to submit a DNA sample? We could use it to eliminate you as a suspect."

Marvin hesitated.

"I suppose it wouldn't hurt."

"Thank you. I'll collect that before we leave. What decision did you reach at your family meeting?"

"Peter agreed to check into a private investigator. Lawrence lives across the street from the Armstrongs. He planned to keep an eye on Connie."

"Did your son hire someone?"

"He'd chosen one. Had an appointment with him this week."

"Your daughter has already answered this question. Where were you on Tuesday?"

"Home, with my wife. We worked in the garden all day."

"Can anyone verify that?"

"She took several phone calls, but I didn't talk to anybody."

"Do you own any rifles?"

"This is Wyoming. Everyone owns rifles."

"Thank you. We'll need to talk to your son now. Thank you for your time, Mrs. Weller."

Marvin led Garret and Tony to the back yard, where a younger, shorter version of himself pushed two children on a swing. Marvin waved the visitors to a stop and took his son's place. Everett Marvin joined Garret and Tony.

"Dad says you need to ask me some questions."

"This won't take long, Mr. Marvin. Your father has told us about the family meeting to discuss your brother-in-law's affair. Did you pass that information along to anyone?"

"Um-m. Not exactly."

"Not exactly?"

"I was letting off steam to one of my friends. You know, about Jason. He said that everybody knows Jason's a jerk. I told him this was different. Something new. He wanted to hear more, but I clammed up."

"I see. Where were you on Tuesday?"

"At home. Sleeping. I work nights."

"Can anyone verify your whereabouts?"

"No."

"Did you work Monday and Tuesday night?"

"Tuesday. Not Monday."

"Thank you, Mr. Marvin. We'll be in touch if we have any more questions."

***

It took Garret and Tony the rest of the day, with time out for lunch, to speak to everyone in the Marvin family who knew of the affair. They interviewed the other three Marvin siblings, learning that all had shared the news with their spouses.   One of Mrs. Weller's brothers and a brother-in-law had an alibi for the day of the murder.

Garret drove the Yukon out of Jackson just after four. He cast a glance Tony's way.

"Pretty exciting stuff, huh?"

"Dull, but interesting."

"How can it be both?"

"I learned a lot watching you. Same questions, but different delivery for different people."

"Did you learn anything from the suspects?"

"They're all glad he's dead. They're a close family, so they all had motive. The evidence ruled out a female shooter, right?"

"The suspect weighed in at two hundred pounds or more with a size ten or eleven shoe. None of the Marvin women are that big."

"Did we figure out the height from the spot where he laid?"

"Less than six feet."

"That rules out the patriarch. Both Everett and Lawrence stand about five-eight, five-nine. And neither of them have an alibi."

"You're getting the hang of this routine police work."

"You're a good teacher."

"Jeez, don't tell anybody."

By the time they reached their motel, the other agents had gathered in the conference room. Garret asked for reports.

Both the former business partner and competition had alibis for the day of the murder.

Dimaggio shed more light on the affair.

"Weller's mistress is Connie Armstrong. Didn't think her husband knew about the affair. Wrong. He knew and has no alibi for the day of the murder."

"Don't these people have jobs? We can usually eliminate suspects on weekdays." Garret said. "I suppose, like everyone else, he owns rifles."

"A wall full."

Garret tapped a pen on the table. As the silence dragged on, Tony spoke.

"How tall is he?"

Dimaggio hit his forehead with the heel of his hand and swore in Itallian.

"He must be six-four. Cross off the jealous husband."

Garret, fighting a smile, swivelled to face Tony.

"That would have come to us eventually. We *are* trained professionals. Don't get a big head."

Tony raised his eyebrows and placed his palm on his chest.

"Me?"

"Probably not something we have to worry about. So our two prime suspects are Lawrence and Everett Marvin. We need more than motive and height for search warrants. Egan, do we have a report on the trace evidence from the crime scene?"

"Not yet."

"Light a fire under the lab. And get that swab from Mrs. Weller's father on its way tonight. If we get trace for comparison, that will tell us if the killer is or isn't a member of that family. Tomorrow, we talk to everybody in Jackson if we have to. If we can't get some trace, we need a witness who heard one of these people threaten to kill Weller. Or something to get us a warrant."

***

"I miss you."

"Tony!" Kelly said. "I miss you. Where are you?"

"Sitting on the porch of this really neat motel. It's a log cabin. Very rustic."

"Grand Teton? We heard about a murder up there."

"Yeah."

"Here's Brett."

"Hi, Daddy. Are you still helping the FBI?"

"Yeah. It's pretty interesting. But I miss you."

"I miss you too, Daddy. I didn't miss you before, because I didn't know you. I want you to come home."

Tony swallowed.

"It'll only be a few more days. I like being with you more than anything in the world. But grownups have to work. We can't be with our kids all the time."

"I know."

"I love you, son."

"I love you, Daddy."

"Let me talk to your mom for a little bit, then we'll talk some more."

"Okay."

Kelly came back on the line.

"I thought we'd hear from you before now."

"I'm sorry. The first night, we were in the mountains. Last night, I was so exhausted, I didn't even eat supper. Today was a lot easier. We're going to eat in a few minutes."

"Garret working you hard?"

"Yesterday. This is really educational. It'll come in handy if I get that job."

"Think positive. When you get that job."

"Yeah. I promised Brett I'd talk to him some more. I'll try to call again tomorrow night."

He told Brett about his motel, the view, and the weather. He answered his son's questions, then disconnected with a sigh.

"It's tough being away from your kid," Garret said from the open door.

Tony nodded.

"I've already missed so much."

"My kid's sixteen. I've probably missed half the important events in his life. It's a credit to my wife that he's turned out as good as he did. You have your priorities straight, Tony."

"I just wish . . . we were a family. We are. But, I mean . . ."

"Do you love her?"

"I think so. I've never been in love. What do I know?"

"Haven't you had training? Don't ministers council people about these things?"

"Yeah. It's a lot tougher when you're the one making the decision."

Garret laughed.

"You think? Doubts don't mean that you don't love her. Almost everybody has doubts."

Tony's smile started slowly, progressing to a full-fledged grin.

"A very wise pastor told me the same thing about choosing my vocation."

"I swear. First a teacher, then a minister. You see things in me that nobody else sees. I think you're touched in the head."

"Or you're showing me a side you don't let most people see."

Garret stared at the mountains for a moment.

"You got me there." He turned his gaze on Tony. "In this business I don't run into people who are so open and honest. Even my own people have an agenda. Usually ambition. You're just Tony. Doing everything you can to help other people. Asking for nothing but a word of thanks or praise. You bring out the mentor in me."

Tony shrugged.

"It's not like I'm not getting paid for this."

"You'd be getting paid the same thing for a lot less work back at Evergreen. And you wouldn't have to be away from your kid. If you'd said 'no', I could have gotten someone else."

"I'm not indispensable?"

"None of us are. Let's go eat."

"Okay. And I really appreciate the mentoring."

"Thank me by saying 'yes' the next time I call."

***

The following morning, Garret had a new strategy. He enlightened his team during a breakfast meeting.

"Let's see if we can use all those forensics shows on TV to our advantage. The average citizen thinks we can get DNA results almost instantly. And they have no idea what we can prove with DNA evidence. We bring Everett and Lawrence Marvin in to separate interrogation rooms. Tell them both we have a–oh, let's say–eight point match between DNA from their old man and trace evidence left by the shooter."

Garret drank coffee and Dimaggio chuckled.

"Sounds impressive. Eight point match. They don't know it's bull."

"Exactly. We tell them it proves the shooter was a male Marvin. We add a little truth to the mix. The height and weight evidence. Tell them as soon as the warrant arrives, we'll collect their DNA and prove they're the shooter. Say it will go easier on them if they confess. The hairs we collected at the crime scene will give us all this in a few days. I'm just tired of wasting my time here when we could be working on our primary case."

Heads nodded around the table.

"Don't forget to read them their rights. Treat them like a suspect. But I spring this on them after they've had some time to sweat. Phillips, Egan, arrange for two rooms at the Jackson police station. Dimaggio, Ferguson, pick up Lawrence. Vasquez, Finch, you have Everett. When you have both of them located, pick them up at the same time. Don't let them see each other. Let's go."

***

Again, Garret allowed Tony to accompany him. He gave very simple instructions. Stand against the wall behind him and look grim. Tony thought he could handle the assignment.

They first confronted a glowering Lawrence. Garret delivered his discourse, brandishing a printout showing two DNA samples.

Lawrence's glower disappeared and he did not allow Garret to finish.

"Someone in my family murdered Jason?"

"Oh, that's priceless acting. The surprise almost seems genuine."

"I'm shocked. I just can't imagine anyone in my family resorting to that. You don't need a warrant. I know I didn't kill Jason. I'll volunteer my DNA."

"Convenient, since you know the warrant is coming."

"You can even hold me till you get the results, if it'll make you feel better. I have nothing to hide."

Garret stood.

"I'll send an agent in to collect the sample." Tony followed him from the room. "That went well, don't you think?"

"Everett could be the guilty party."

"Let's hope so."

They found Everett sweating and fidgeting. Garret's delivery remained the same, like a predator going for the jugular. But the difference in the suspect's attitude boosted Tony's adrenalin output. To give his nervous hands something to do, he began fingering the crucifix he wore.

Everett's eyes darted to him several times while Garret gave his speech.

"What do you say, Everett? Once we get the positive match, you won't be in a position to cut a deal. It'll go easier on you if you confess."

"Okay. No death penalty, right."

"If you cooperate fully."

"Okay. Just make him stop that."

Garret turned in his chair, as surprised as Tony.

"You mean that thing with the cross?"

"Yeah." He addressed Tony. "How'd you know how guilty I feel? I've had all I could do not to go to confession. I'm not a cold-blooded killer. I just didn't want him to hurt my sister any more."

Tony let his hand drop and said nothing, trying for a neutral expression. Garret answered the question.

"We call him 'the Reverend.' He attended the seminary before he came to work for us. He knows a man with a guilty conscience when he sees one."

Everett hung his head and Tony bit his lip to deflect a smile.

Ferguson and Dimaggio entered the room to record Everett's confession. When Tony and Garret reached the hall, they both smiled. Garret slapped his back.

"Thanks for the help."

"I know a guilty conscience when I see one? I just got excited when I saw how nervous he was. I had to do something with my hand."

"Whatever works. Don't forget that trick. It'll only work on the few who have religion and a guilty conscience. But we'll take whatever advantage we can get. How'd you like to go home?"

"Yeah. I would."

"Most of the team can take off this afternoon. You'll be home for supper. I'll be in touch."

***

One of the deputies took Tony from the airport back to Spruce Lake, explaining that the last FBI agent had left town. Knowing that Kelly would still be at work, Tony asked for a ride to the ranger station.

Don saw him first.

"Ah-h! The prodigal son returns!"

Kelly looked up from her paperwork with a smile that brightened the room. Tony grinned as she rushed to him. Mindful of the audience, they did not kiss. But he picked her up when they hugged. Don and Red laughed. Red made the first comment.

"Get a room."

"Shame on you, Red," Don said. "You're talking about the Reverend. Tell him to get a ring."

"Oh, yeah."

Tony, gazing into Kelly's eyes, tried to ignore them. He did not want to speak the words in front of an audience, but he could hold them in no longer. He whispered.

"I love you."

Kelly's eyes glistened.

"What'd he say?" Don asked.

"The L word," Red replied.

Don clapped his hands once.

"It's about time!"

"Shut up, Don," Tony said. "I'll be back to work tomorrow morning."

"Don't change the subject."

Tony wrapped one arm around Kelly's shoulders and kissed her forehead before facing Don.

"If you don't want to talk about work, I haven't seen my son in four days."

"Okay. Okay. I heard there was an arrest up in Wyoming. Have you rid the national parks of a serial killer?"

"I'm afraid not. It was a copy cat."

"Damn. I hope they get this guy soon. He's keeping people away from parks all over the country."

"They only people who need to worry are the macho types who hike alone."

"We know that, but everybody gets scared."

***

Tony fumbled for the phone.

"Hullo."

"Wake up. I have work for you."

"Garret?"

"Do I have to call you back after your first cup of coffee?"

"No." Tony sat up and looked at his alarm clock. Four-twenty. "I'm awake. Another killing?"

"Yeah. Glacier again."

"Well, I got to spend three days at home anyhow."

"Get packed. We'll be wheels up in an hour and a quarter. I'll have a deputy pick you up at 0530."

"Have him pick me up at Kelly's place. I need to say goodbye to Brett."

"And Kelly."

Garret disconnected. Tony began jamming clothes into the duffle bag which still sat on his dresser, grateful that he had showered the night before. He rushed to the kitchen, jammed the button on his coffee maker, then struggled into his clothes. He drank his first cup while lacing on his boots.

"Cell phone!"

After clipping it to his belt, he threw the charger into his bag. A quick trip to the bathroom added his shaving kit to the collection. Finally, he squeezed in his daily devotional book. He filled his thermal mug, pulled on his jacket, and hurried out the door. Then returned for his duffle bag.

Checking the time as he climbed the stairs, he sighed and retrieved his watch. Four-fifty. He hoped that Kelly would not object too much to an awakening before sunrise. He hurried through patchy fog and tapped softly on her door at five AM.

To his astonishment, the light came on momentarily. She did not seem surprised to see him.

"Were you expecting me?"

"No. But I woke up a half-hour ago and just had this feeling I shouldn't go back to sleep. I guess you're leaving town."

"Yeah. Glacier this time."

She hugged him.

"I'm really beginning to hate this."

"I know. But it's temporary. And it's good experience for me."

She pulled him down for a long kiss.

"Think about that while you're gone."

He grinned.

"I think about that all the time. When I get back, we need to talk about our future."

"Oh. Our future?"

"Yeah."

"I'd like that."

"Good. How grumpy do you think Brett will be if I wake him up?"

"He'll go back to sleep. He'd be real upset if you didn't say goodbye to him. Go ahead."

***

Tony found himself less excited on this flight, but still unable to sleep. After he studied the preliminary report and contour maps, he read his devotion and ate the breakfast bar.

The pilot announced their descent to the Babb, Montana airport.

People woke, put things away, and fastened their seatbelts. Before the plane stopped, Garret stood, barking orders as he worked his way to the door. Two SUVs took them south on Highway 89 to St. Mary and park headquarters, where they would meet the local authorities.

Remembering what Garret had said about the unsub staying to watch, Tony looked around before entering the ranger station. A chill ran up his spine. He searched for the source of his discomfort and focused on a departing, filthy, dark green pickup with what appeared to be Wyoming plates.

"You look like you've seen a ghost," Garret said.

"It's probably nothing. But I have a feeling about that pickup."

"Phillips. Egan. Check out that dark green truck."

They jumped into one of the SUVs and backed out of the parking place, squealing tires. The pickup turned a corner four blocks away. Enough traffic clogged the small town street to keep them from speeding to catch up.

"Probably a wild goose chase," Tony said.

"I believe in hunches, Tony. What got your attention?"

"I don't know. It passed while we were getting out. I just had a real bad feeling."

"Did you see the driver?"

Tony frowned.

"I must have. But I don't remember anything about him."

"It may come to you. Did you get the license plate?"

"It was too dirty. But I'm pretty sure I saw the Wyoming bronco."

"What else?"

"At least a ten-year-old Ford, with a shell, topper, whatever you want to call it. Painted green, not quite as dark as the pickup."

"Anybody see anything different?"

"The back door of the shell was missing," Dimaggio said.

Tony nodded.

"Let's go talk to the authorities," Garret ordered.

They all entered a conference room to meet with the Glacier County sheriff, a Montana state trooper, and Glacier's head ranger. The state trooper had new lab reports. The ranger informed them that a helicopter would pick them up whenever they were ready.

"The chopper can haul seven plus the pilot. How many of my people will you need?"

"None. We'll want to talk to anyone who was on the scene or anyone who talked to the victim. But that can be done here."

"Do your people know a lot about operating in the back country?"

"Mr. Wagner is our back country expert. I'm confident in his ability. Vasquez, find out what's taking Phillips and Egan so long." He continued talking to the local authorities until Vasquez reported that he could not raise either agent's cell phone. Garret's eyebrows met. "Use the GPS to locate them."

Vasquez used his computer while the room fell silent.

"They're stationary on Fewer Road, about a mile off Highway 89."

"Sheriff, send a unit out there."

The sheriff spoke into his radio.

"4263, what's your twenty?"

"Just coming out of Johnson's Restaurant."

"Get out to Fewer Road, about a mile off 89. We can't raise two FBI agents." They heard a siren outside the building. The sheriff explained. "You might have noticed Johnson's across the street when you came in. What else should I tell them, Agent Garret?"

"Use extreme caution. The agents were driving a Yukon and investigating a dark green, older model Ford truck."

The sheriff frowned and passed the information along. The only sound in the room came from the coffee maker as it brewed another pot. Tony said a silent prayer. The radio crackled.

"We're pulling up to the Yukon. No other vehicle in sight." Garret paced. The silence wore on. "Send an ambulance to our location! Two officers down!"

Garret swore. Chaos erupted. Garret bolted for the door.

"Tony, Vasquez, stay here! Get an APB out on that truck. Sheriff, take us there!"

***

Tony and Vasquez tried to study the evidence with little success. Tony decided to try conversation.

"Does this get any easier?"

"I wouldn't know. This is the first time anybody I know's been shot."

"Me too. I know Phillips a little better than Egan."

"He has a habit of screwing up. He's usually in Garret's dog house."

Tony nodded.

"He made me haul a backpack a hundred feet up a cliff because he dropped the cargo line."

Vasquez smiled.

"No one lets him drive. He rear-ended another vehicle once because he was so intent on his suspect."

"His heart's in the right place."

"Yeah."

Vasquez's phone rang. He listened in silence, finally said "Okay" and disconnected.

"Egan's dead. Phillip's has a head wound and probably won't make it." He bit his lip. "Their vehicle was still running, but in park. They were shot through the windshield."

Tony turned away. *If I'd taken my feeling more seriously, they might have been more cautious. I can't blame myself. This guy knows how to protect himself. The pickup cab probably had a sliding window. With no back door in the topper, he had a clear shot. They probably didn't even see him. I did all I could.*

Now he only felt useless. *I'd be better off in the park, looking for evidence.*

"Tony, we need to set up a command post here. The ranger has her hands full. Give me a hand."

"Just tell me what to do."

"We'll use all the available space. I'll box and seal the evidence, to get it out of our way. She'll show you where to find the crisis supplies. Start by adding more signs out front for official vehicles. She's calling in extra help. When they get here, look official and tell them to report to me. If anyone asks any questions, tell them you're not at liberty to say."

"Got it."

After Tony placed the signs, Vasquez gave additional orders.

"Find phone books, phone lists, maps, notepads, pens. Put the maps in the center of the conference table, a half-dozen of each of the others around the table. Make sure each of the desks has everything but maps." A phone rang and Vasquez shouted. "Anybody official, refer to me. Anybody else, tell them 'no comment.' Got that?"

"Yeah. But what if one of our family members have heard that someone was shot."

"Tell them it wasn't anyone local."

The ranger answered the phone.

"It's the State Police."

Vasquez took the call.

***

An air ambulance transported Phillips to a Missoula hospital. At 6:45 that evening, he died. By that time, members of the state police, border patrol, park service, and sheriff's department packed the ranger station. The media gathered outside. Tony fetched supplies, made coffee, and passed out food after one of the deputies returned from Johnson's Restaurant.

"What kind of an FBI agent are you?" the deputy asked.

"I'm not. I'm a consultant. They don't need my expertise for this. I was brought along to go into the back country."

"Oh."

A new face arrived and Garret hurried to greet him. Garret never *met* anyone. He let them come to him. He waved to Tony, who washed his sandwich down with coffee on his way across the room.

"Tony, this is Dr. Harris, another of our consultants. One of his skills is hypnosis. I want him to see if you can remember more under hypnosis."

"O-kay."

"You're a skeptic," Dr. Harris said.

"Yeah."

"But you'll do anything you can to help?"

"Of course."

"Then try to dispel your skepticism in the interest of helping."

Tony nodded and followed them into the head ranger's office. With the door closed and the lights dim, he concentrated on the doctor's soothing voice.

"You are standing in front of the ranger station and a green truck approaches. What do you see?"

"I didn't turn around till it was right beside me."

"Can you see into the cab?"

"Yes. It's dark."

"Can you see the driver?"

"No. He's in shadows."

"You can't see his face. But think, Tony. You can tell something from his features."

"He's a big man. Big arms. Big hands. His face isn't in profile. He's looking at me. He saw me!"

"You are very calm, Tony. He cannot harm you. Now, describe his vehicle."

"Dark green, probably a forest green. Ford. Probably fifteen years old. Dent just behind the passenger side door. Been on some muddy roads. Real dirty. Black dirt. Green topper. Not a factory color. Brush marks."

"What shade of green?"

"Kelly maybe."

"What else about the topper?"

"Cracked passenger side window."

"Okay. Now the truck has passed. You're looking at the back of the truck. What do you see?"

"More dirt. But the door of the topper is missing. The pickup has a sliding rear window. I can see the light through it."

"Tell me about the license plate."

"Dirty. But there's a horse. Wyoming."

"Letters? Numbers?"

"No-o. It's really dirty."

"Tell me more."

"The right side of the bumper is bent down a little. Mud flaps, with no markings."

Dr. Harris turned to Garret.

"I think he's given you all he can."

"Wake him up. I want you to try this on a couple of my agents. We all saw that truck. Maybe one of 'em can remember the plate number."

"Tony, you will wake calm and relaxed, remembering everything that you said."

He snapped his fingers. Tony lifted his head and looked at Garret.

"Did that help?"

"Some. It's a long shot, but this guy has the same build as the hiker you saw in Evergreen."

"He looked right at me. That must be why I got scared."

"And he thinks you saw him. He's probably cleared out of here. But just to be safe, you don't leave here without a shadow. And we don't want you on camera. I'm sending you to the motel for some sleep. Take the jacket and ID off before you leave. In the morning, you and Finch will take a couple rangers into the park to continue the initial investigation. That's where you can do the most good. And it'll keep you out of the public eye."

"I've felt pretty useless around here. I'd rather do something. I know I'm safe with you guys. What about when I go home?"

"He thinks you're an FBI agent. And now we can assume he's from Wyoming. He won't know where to look for you."

***

This crime scene lay at a higher elevation than the one in Evergreen. Rockier terrain and fewer trees made tracking even more difficult. The killer had chosen one of the few patches of dense cover for his initial ambush. Tony studied the tracks and questioned one of the rangers.

"Is this the trail where the other guy was killed?"

"Yeah. But he didn't come up as high last time."

They followed the same procedure as they had at Evergreen. Based on maps and what he could see, Tony guessed which route the killer would use for his escape. He asked the two rangers their opinions. His assessment agreed with theirs. Finch told the rangers what to look for and they fanned out along the possible trail.

Tony chose the route nearest the drop off–not a cliff, but a 45 to 70 degree rock slope, full of cracks and pockets. Over the centuries, soil had collected in these and plants had taken root–some grasses, a few twisted trees, but mainly juniper shrubs. If the killer had thrown a backpack here, it would be difficult to find. And this victim had carried a navy blue backpack, making the task even harder. Tony spent as much time scanning the slope as he did the ground in front of him. He carried his equipment bag rather than sending someone back to the helicopter if he needed it.

They combed the ground for three hours, finding nothing. Finch called a lunch break and consulted with Tony.

"Your opinion?"

"I think we've gone far enough. I'd suggest heading back, with all of us concentrating on the slope. He doesn't take long to get rid of the backpack. I'd bet it's down there somewhere."

"Makes sense to me."

As they worked their way back, Tony formed an opinion which he kept to himself. The killer would have picked one of the steep slopes to dispose of the backpack, because it would travel farther. *I don't want to influence them if I'm wrong. This is like finding a needle in a haystack.*

"Is that it?" one of the rangers said, looking through his binoculars.

"Where?" Tony asked before raising his glasses.

"Right in front of the biggest pine, in the scrub juniper."

Tony used his binoculars. A patch of navy in the dark green junipers. He unpacked his bag. Though less strenuous than the climb in Evergreen, it had it's own challenges. Negotiating the rocks and brush would take time. He would have to carry the pack. Dragging it up in a cargo net could cause too much damage.

He anchored his rope and tied himself off, then descended facing forward, wanting to see his route. He used the rope only as a safety line. He skirted as much of the juniper as he could, knowing it hid many irregularities. He also zigzagged to avoid loose rocks.

Tony lost his footing, landing flat on his back in the prickly juniper.

Flat? That's a relative term on a 50 degree slope. He simply leaned forward on the rope to regain his feet. *What's this?* The shrubs hid more than he had anticipated. *I couldn't have reached the backpack without a rope.*

He peered over the precipice, only about fifteen feet, but a nasty surprise for a free climber. The anomaly extended seventy-five yards to his right and a hundred to his left, gradually tapering to nothing. The whole hillside had sloughed, maybe in an ancient earthquake. He took a closer look at the terrain and let his breath out. *Nothing's moved in decades.* No need to worry about the rock giving way beneath him.

The greatest difficulty in this descent lay in the angle of the cliff. Not ninety degrees, at least a hundred. *The descent isn't the problem. I didn't bring my aiders down.* He considered going back for them, decided against it, then turned and backed over the edge. He lowered himself to the slope. *If it had landed here, we never would've found it. Thank you, Lord.*

He fell into the juniper once more before reaching the backpack. After tying off his safety line, he collected the evidence. When he had it securely bagged and netted, he checked the ground around it, looking for anything which might have fallen out. Satisfied that he had missed nothing, he hooked the net over his shoulder and began walking up.

Tony eyed the cliff. *You climbed a longer rope in high school gym class. Just keep telling yourself that.* He tied the net to the rope a few feet below him, wrapped his leg in the line, and heaved himself up. Hand over hand. Five feet. Ten feet. *There's the top. Almost there. It'll be easier when I can get a foot hold.*

His hands slipped. He gripped harder and the skid stopped. He hated doing things over. Ten feet. Eleven. Twelve. Feet planted. *Just walk up. One step at a time.*

He crawled over the edge and fell face-first into the juniper, arms throbbing, lungs protesting.

"You okay!" Finch.

Tony raised his hand and waved once. He rested until Finch inquired again. Tony pushed himself to his hands and knees.

"I'm coming!"

He retrieved his cargo and finished the climb. Not nearly as exhausted as he had been in Evergreen, he still let the others collect his gear. Finch picked up the backpack.

"Garret wouldn't want us to come back without this."

"No one found the backpack last fall," a ranger offered.

"No one has found most of them. He's not very happy about that."

"He doesn't have much to be happy about right now," Tony said. "Glad we can offer something positive. Would you guys try something for me? Pick up that pack to see how much it weighs. Then pick up a rock about the same weight. See how far you can throw it. I'd do it myself, but my arms are rubbery."

Finch nodded.

"I see what you're getting at. It'd probably take a pretty strong guy to get it that far."

Each of the three threw a rock. One managed to bounce over the precipice.

"Granted the aerodynamics of a rock and a backpack are different," Tony said.

"But the backpack wouldn't move as far once it hit. Our unsub is one powerful guy. That's a useful piece of information. Let's get back to civilization."

***

Garret listened to Finch's report, dark brows above his eyes, dark circles below. He had not slept since coming to Glacier.

"Good work, both of you. Finch, come back after you get that evidence ready for transport."

Finch left them alone. Tony sighed.

"I wish I could have done more."

"We've been really busy the past day, but more than one agent told me you did all you could. We appreciate it. And that bit with the rocks. That's using your head. You said the guy had big arms and hands. This supports your eyewitness testimony."

"Eyewitness. Will I have to testify?"

"If the guy makes it to trial, I think you can count on it. He may not be tried for all the murders, but you can bet he'll go before a judge for killing two FBI agents."

"If he makes it to trial?"

"He killed two FBI agents. Hellfire. If he gives me an excuse, I'll blow him away. I'm sure some of these guys are even more eager to save the taxpayers an expensive trial."

"I understand."

Finch returned.

"Good. Now, Tony, Finch's going to teach you everyone's favorite part of the job. Paperwork. I want a report from you on what happened today. He'll give you some guidelines, then he'll correct it. You shouldn't have to rewrite it more than three or four times. Facts and observations, not opinions. Any questions?"

"Can I get something to eat first?"

"Yeah. You can even work on it at your motel room after a shower. Just have it done by noon tomorrow. Don't think I'm giving you the bum's rush, but you're headed home about one. You've done your job. I want you out of here in case our unsub is still lurking."

"Okay. Am I flying again?"

"Yeah. We're sending evidence to our lab. They can make a detour for you. Finch, stick with Tony. Remember, he's the only person alive who's seen our unsub."

"Yes, sir."

***

The plane touched down just after sunset. Ryan waited for him in his department pickup. When Tony climbed in, the sheriff grinned.

"Pretty fancy ride. Getting to be a mighty important man when the FBI tells me to come fetch you from the airport."

"Oh, knock it off. Garret just wants a rock climber he trusts."

"You were up in Glacier then."

"Yeah."

"Nasty business. They haven't released the agents names. Anybody I knew?"

"You know I'm not supposed to say."

"I'll keep my mouth shut."

"Phillips."

"Young fella. Garret didn't like him much."

"Yeah."

"What a shame. They were chasing a suspect?"

"Following. And they probably didn't take it seriously. Garret sent them based on my hunch."

"Your hunch?"

"I feel pretty bad about that."

"Garret's a heck of an investigator. If he trusted your hunch, they should have. It's not your fault."

"Thanks, Ryan."

"They broadcast a description of that pickup clear down here. Don't
see how he can get away."

"He's smart and he knows the back country. They've never found a
track anywhere. And you know how much ground the crime scenes cover.
I'll bet he has topographic maps showing all the back roads. The FBI
checked them around Glacier, but away from there law enforcement is
looking on the highways."

"Most likely. Unless some over-enthusiastic deputy gets hold of it."

"I hope not. A wet-behind-the-ears deputy is no match for this guy."

"Hardly."

"Take me to Kelly's place." Ryan raised his eyebrows. "And don't
say a word about it to anyone."

"Don't need to. One of the neighbors will notice."

"Drop me a block away."

Ryan grinned.

"Sneaking around! I'm disillusioned."

"Too bad. Hopefully, before the summer's over, I can quit caring
what other people think."

"Planning some changes?"

"Yeah. And, no, I'm not telling you what they are."

Ryan laughed and left him by the city park a block from Kelly's
apartment.

"Remember, you have to go to church on Sunday."

"Go away."

Tony saw no one between there and his destination. He knocked
softly, knowing that Brett would be in bed. Kelly peered through the

window before flinging the door open. She spoke in excited whispers.

"I'm so glad you're back. I was really worried when I heard what happened."

He closed the door and pulled her into his arms. Neither of them talked for some time. Finally, he needed to breath.

"I love you. . . Will you marry me?"

"Yes."

He grinned.

"I don't want to wait. I want to marry you yesterday."

"Shouldn't we give our parents a chance to come."

He sighed.

"If that means telling them before we do it, yeah. If it means waiting until they can fit it into their schedules, no. I'm miserable. Not just physically. I missed both of you when I was gone. I want to sleep under the same roof with you every night."

"You could move in with us. We wouldn't have to sleep together."

"No. I can't. I don't care what everyone thinks of me. But I do care what some people think. I can't ask too much of them."

"I love how much you care. Stay tonight. You can sleep on the couch. I'll set the alarm so you can leave before it's light."

"Okay. I want to see Brett."

They walked to his bedroom door, holding hands. He slipped his arm around her as he watched his son sleep. She kissed his cheek.

"I love you, Tony."

"I love you." They returned to the livingroom and shared another long kiss on the couch. When their passion became too intense, they separated. "We should see the pastor tomorrow."

"Should we call our parents tonight?"

"Um-m. Yes and no."

"I think I should call my parents to give them as much notice as possible."

"What do they think of me?"

"They're kind of amazed that Brett's father turned out to be such a nice guy."

"Go ahead and call. But I'm too tired to talk to them."

"Chicken."

"That too."

"You're not going to call your parents?"

"I'm too tired. I'll call them after I go home in the morning. They're early risers."

***

Tony made it to his apartment before daylight, showered, then called his parents. Having seen him with Kelly, they were less surprised than her parents. But the quick wedding shocked them.

"Tony, don't rush into this," Amanda said.

"Mom, the past three months have hit me like an avalanche. Kelly's been here for me the whole time. It doesn't feel like rushing. It feels like finally."

Mike cleared his throat.

"How much of the 'finally' is physical?"

"Some. When I saw Kelly this spring, I was scared of her. But she's not the same girl who seduced me. She's the kind of woman I had started looking for."

"When? I didn't think you were looking."

"After Kelly showed up and the pastor told me I needed a wife."

"Does this mean you're giving up the seminary?"

"Oh. Still not sure about that. I've applied for a permanent job here.
I figure if the Lord wants me to quit, I'll get the job."

"And if you go back to school, what will she do?"

"Oh. Guess we haven't talked about that."

"You'd better. And if you become a minister, you'll need to relocate."

"Oh."

"Maybe you'd better slow down a little."

"We'll have a long talk tonight. I'd better get ready for work."

After disconnecting, Tony sighed. *I don't want to go back to school.
I don't want to be a minister. I don't like crowds. I like being alone in the
woods.*

"How many years have I ignored that?"

At the end of every college day he had rushed into the woods for
solitude. *I'll make a lot better park ranger than a pastor.* He felt like a
weight had been lifted from him.

"Lord, you tried to tell me all along. I just wasn't listening."

He finished dressing and bounded up the steps and around the corner
of the house.

"Morning, Tony."

He jumped sideways.

"Gil! You scared the living daylights out of me."

"Hanging out with the FBI making you jumpy? I drink my coffee on
the deck more often than not."

"I didn't know you were back. And I'm preoccupied with better
things. Kelly said she'd marry me!"

"No kidding! If Betty'd known she'd of told me. For once, I get to
tell her some news."

"Wait until this evening. Once she knows, it'll be all over town."

"Okay. I'll keep it a secret if you tell me what you've been up to. Glacier's been all over the news. Were you up there?"

"Yeah. I'd rather think about the great stuff happening here."

"Quite a tragedy. Were you there when those agents got killed?"

Tony nodded. "Heard on the news they're looking for an old, green pickup. Did anyone see the driver?"

"I'll tell you. But you can't tell Betty."

Gil leaned foreword.

"Promise."

"I sort of saw him. But even under hypnosis, I couldn't remember anything except he had big arms."

Gil sat back.

"Huh. Thought that was supposed to make you remember everything."

"Everything I saw. It was dark inside the pickup. I couldn't see the guy."

"Too bad. Someone needs to stop this guy."

"Yeah. Just don't spread around what I saw. Everybody will start watching my back if they know. I shouldn't have told you."

"You've known me a lot of years, Tony. I can keep a secret. Now telling Betty would have been dumb. You go on to work and don't worry about me blabbing."

"Thanks, Gil. If I want to keep working with the FBI I'd better learn to keep my mouth shut."

Gil just laughed.

***

Pastor Johnson frowned at Tony and Kelly, sitting in his study.

"I question your motivation. Why the rush?"

Tony blushed.

"Yes. There's physical motivation. That's part of the reason for the rush. But it's not the reason we want to get married. We love each other."

The pastor's frown deepened.

"Have you discussed your future? Children? Career?"

"We did that today. This morning, I admitted to myself that I don't want to be a minister. I'm much happier in the woods. I've applied for a year round job here. We'd like at least one more child."

"Kelly, what do you have to say?"

"For me, Tony was the one that got away. I never forgot him. I wanted the chance to get to know him better, to see if my first impression was accurate. He hasn't disappointed me."

"But he will. Everyone disappoints us at some point. What then?"

She chewed her lip.

"I love him. I hope, if he disappoints me, I can remember that we're all human. Either he made a mistake, or I expected too much, or both."

The pastor stroked his chin for so long that Tony began to fidget.

"You've talked to your parents?" They both nodded. "When did you have in mind?"

"Next Saturday morning," Tony said.

"Morning?"

"We just have the weekend off. We want to make the most of it."

"I see. What time?"

"Ten?"

"Good enough. You have a lot of friends. Do you want to invite them?"

Tony looked at Kelly.

"I hadn't planned on it. Pastor, what do you think?"

"Your friends will be really disappointed. All those people who kept a vigil outside the jail for you. They deserve the chance to come."

"Yeah. But they need to know it's nothing fancy. No reception. We're getting married, then we're out of there."

"I'll put an announcement in the bulletin, and announce it after the service on Sunday. The congregation will take care of the rest of the town. You might tell some of your closest friends. And perhaps a best man and maid-of-honor."

"Oh."

"We hadn't thought of that," Kelly said.

"Give it some consideration," Pastor Johnson advised. "And speak to one of the organists about providing music. I'll see about ushers for you. Come back Monday evening. We'll have another talk."

They left, holding hands, not talking for several blocks. Kelly squeezed his hand.

"Now we get to tell Brett."

"He'll love it, because I'll be living with you. I don't think it's bothered him that we're not married. Just that I don't live with you."

"Yeah. My parents said they'd come. I want my mom for matron-of-honor."

"That's nice. Dad's haying. But he said Mom could come. I thought I'd ask Don. He's helped this thing along. And I really think he's my best friend here."

"I thought so."

"Let's get this all out of the way tonight. We'll tell Brett, get something to eat, go see Don, then Ethel. She'll be our organist. We have to find some time to get rings."

"We have Monday off."

"That'll have to work. Let's call our parents right now. We got a couple more blocks to walk."

They both used their cell phones. Tony reached his parents voice mail and left a message with the day and time of their wedding. Kelly spoke to her mother. Judging by her happy tears, she had her matron-of-honor. She had not finished talking when they reached the babysitter's house.

Brett ran out to greet them and Tony picked him up.

"Why's Mommy crying?"

"She's really happy."

Kelly disconnected.

"I'm so happy, honey. Your daddy and I are getting married."

"Really! When?"

"A week from Saturday."

"Then you can live with us, Daddy?"

"Yes. But that will mean some changes."

"What kind?"

"Your mom and I will sleep with the bedroom door closed."

"Why?"

"We need some time alone. We love you. So if you need us at night, you'll have to knock on our door. Can you handle that?"

"Guess so. I'm getting big now."

"Yes, you are. After we get married, we can get your name changed too."

"To Wagner?"

"Yes."

"Can I tell Cindy?"

"Go ahead." They waited while he told the babysitter, then accepted her congratulations. "We might as well tell everyone we see. It'll be all over town before long anyhow."

"No kidding."

***

"I didn't know there were this many people in Spruce Lake," Tony said to Don, looking into the church.

"I think I recognized a few from out of town. Kelly's parents took a shine to you right away."

"That's a relief."

"And, though you're excused, we're having a reception afterward. Potluck dinner."

Tony grinned.

"Have fun."

"You too. Did your daddy give you the 'how not to get pregnant' lecture?"

Tony blushed.

"I have a box full."

"Good. Don't want to deal with a pregnant employee just now. Going to be tough enough with two of them in love. No sneaking off into the stable for a nooner."

"What about the sleeping room?"

"No procreation on company time."

"Yes, sir."

Pastor Johnson joined them. The organist stopped playing and they walked out into the front of the church. The congregation rose when the processional music began. Brett came first with the rings. Kelly's mother walked down the aisle, followed by Kelly, on her father's arm.

Tony had never seen her in a dress, or more precisely, the western skirt and blouse she had chosen for her wedding dress. She wore baby's breath

in her hair and carried three roses–red, white, and pink. He swallowed
several times. Their eyes met and she smiled, tears on her cheeks. *Good
thing she doesn't wear makeup. She's so beautiful.*

She took his arm and the pastor began.

"Dearly beloved, we are gathered here in the presence of God . . ."

It passed in a blur. Then they left the church, stopping in the entry to
greet their guests. His eyes kept returning to her as the steady stream of
well-wishers passed. It seemed that the town had been left unattended.
Then one guest gained his full attention.

"Garret? How'd you hear about this?"

"I'm the FBI. I hear things."

"Thanks for coming. I wouldn't have expected you if we'd sent an
engraved invitation."

"Probably wouldn't have come then. But if you're crazy enough to
get married this fast, I'm crazy enough to stop on my way through for the
wedding." He kissed Kelly's cheek. "Congratulations. I have a plane to
catch."

They finished their greeting duties, then a carriage took them to
Kelly's apartment. Brett would stay at Tony's apartment with his
grandparents. Tony began undressing even before she locked the door. He
watched her do the same, but kept his distance, for fear they would not
reach the bedroom and his supply of condoms.

She recognized his strategy and motioned for him to follow. He kept
his hands off her until they stood beside the bed. Still, they barely
disturbed the blankets before he finished. He gave a sheepish grin. Neither
of them had expected the first time to take long.

He started again. All the unused passion of the past six years seemed
to come out in the next half-hour. Blankets and pillows ended up on the

floor. The headboard banged against the wall. They finally collapsed together, sweating and gasping. Tony brushed the damp hair off her forehead.

"I love you."

"I love you. And now I remember how much fun you were."

"I've never had this much fun."

"You haven't?"

"I'm married now. Much more fun."

"Um-m. You're right. Let's rest a while and do that again."

"Good plan."

***

The weekend passed that way. They ate and slept only when they had to. Monday morning they woke early to make love again before going to work. Kelly plugged the phone in to check for messages. They dressed and stopped by Tony's apartment to greet Amanda and Brett. Kelly's parents had left so her father could get back to work. Amanda would stay until the next morning.

When they reached the ranger station, Tony poured coffee for both of them.

"It's almost a relief to get back to work. I probably would have killed myself on a two week honeymoon."

Kelly laughed.

"Inexperience. You'll have to learn to pace yourself."

"Yeah. But it's so much *fun*."

He kissed her neck and she giggled.

"Knock it off!" Don said. "I told you, not on company time!"

"Yes, sir."

"I really thought you two would be late this morning."

"Have I ever been late?"

"No. But you were never getting any before. What did you have to stay home for?"

Tony blushed.

"True."

"I'm sure you two didn't see the news this weekend. They found that pickup." Satisfied that he had their undivided attention, he continued. "Up near Cody, Wyoming. Torched."

"They'd still be able to trace it unless he removed the plates and VIN."

"News didn't say anything about that. Said it was badly burned in a remote area. Said the FBI took over and confirmed that it was the vehicle."

"Since I didn't see the plate number, they couldn't have used that to ID it. I'll bet he removed the plates and VIN. He's too smart to leave that kind of evidence."

"*You* didn't see the plates?" Kelly said.

"I have to learn to keep my mouth shut. I saw the pickup. Garret sent those two agents on my hunch. They even hypnotized me to help me remember. I didn't see the driver."

She shuddered.

"You should have told me."

"I didn't want you to worry."

"But he might have seen *you*. You could be in danger."

"No. I was wearing an FBI jacket and name tag. He thinks I'm an agent. Garret said I was only in danger right there at Glacier. He has no way to find me."

"But, Tony, he tried to frame you. He knows what you look like."

None of them could speak for what seemed like minutes. Tony's chest felt tight. Finally, Don broke the silence.

162 Paula F. Winskye

"Call Garret."

Tony nodded and used the phone on his desk. He reached Garret's voice mail, but the phone rang five minutes later.

"You said you have a concern," Garret said. He listened to the revelation. "I know."

"You know!"

"Have you noticed any extra tourists hanging around?"

"Nobody notices tourists unless they ask for help."

"Exactly. Although you didn't make it easy by changing residences. We had Kelly's place under surveillance too. We just consolidated everything."

"You've been watching me?"

"Ever since you came back from Glacier. He may not have recognized you. Out of place. Out of uniform. But we weren't taking any chances."

"Why didn't you tell me?"

"Didn't want you to worry about it. Though I was a little surprised you didn't figure this out sooner."

"Probably denial. I was too scared to make the connection."

"I doubt you're in any danger. If you'd seen him, we'd have his picture plastered all over the news by now. He probably feels safe."

"That makes sense, I guess."

"And, if you'd seen him, we'd have you in protective custody. Two reasons for him not to go back to Spruce Lake so soon."

"Okay. That's reassuring, I guess."

"Try not to worry. We know what we're doing."

"I'll try. How long you plan to keep an eye on me?"

"Until we're sure. I'll let you know when I pull them off."

Tony disconnected and gave Kelly and Don the gist of the

conversation.

"Guess I feel better knowing they made the connection right away. They've been on top of it."

Kelly bit her lip and Don scowled.

"They figured ignorance is bliss."

Tony shrugged.

"When I saw that pickup, I felt scared. I think I made the connection, but couldn't admit it to myself."

"I'm scared now," Kelly said.

He hugged her.

"I know. I'm sorry about this. I want you to feel safe."

"I'll talk to Ryan," Don said. "We'll get more people watching your back." Tony wanted to talk to Don alone. His eyes met Don's. "But enough of this. If he hasn't showed up by now, he probably won't. We have work to do."

Kelly nodded.

"I'll feed the cubs."

"Tony, I got some paperwork for you to fill out." They entered Don's office and waited until Kelly left the building. "What is it?"

"This guy doesn't hunt in town. I'm probably safe here. I spend a lot of time in the park."

"I was thinking the same thing. I'll call Garret. Tell him I want some Kevlar for you to wear. Garret's probably right. But let's take every precaution we can."

"Sounds good to me."

"And here's something to help take your mind off that. Your interview's Wednesday morning. He's coming here."

"Oh. You think I should be nervous?"

"Why? This is a piece of cake compared to what you've been through this summer."

"Yeah. It is."

"I've known him for years. I told him I'd be really pissed off if he didn't hire you. Course he wouldn't make any guarantees. Said if someone with more experience applied, he'd probably have to give the job to them. But the seed's been planted."

"Thanks, Don. I really want to stay."

***

The thin Kevlar vest arrived the next day. It fit inconspicuously under Tony's shirt. He felt better. Kelly relaxed visibly. Don's expression lost its grim edge.

On Wednesday, the district supervisor used Don's office for the interview. Tony felt relaxed as the supervisor leafed through his file.

"Peace Officer training with NPS courses from Vermilion. Graduated top of your class. Bachelors in Education from Immanuel Lutheran College. Two point six GPA. Anything you'd like to say about that?"

"I should have read the handwriting on the wall. I got my best grades in courses that would lead to a career working outdoors. I only recently figured that out."

The supervisor smiled and turned a page.

"Your record is pretty spotless. The worst thing Don found to say on any of your evaluations was that you were too soft-spoken. And that was only on the first one. After that, he just wrote that it was hard to find any area where you weren't improving."

"I try to do my best, sir."

"Obviously. This year you spent quite a few days working for the FBI. Thank you for your participation. We promised them our cooperation, but as an individual, you weren't obligated. You made a good impression, based on this letter of recommendation from Agent Wyatt Garret."

"He sent a letter?"

"You didn't ask him to?"

"No, sir."

"Highly unusual recommendation. Agent Garret does not embrace convention. I'll read this to you. 'To whom it may concern. If anything, Tony Wagner is over-qualified for the position of law enforcement ranger. If you don't hire him, I will. The FBI can use someone with his expertise on a full-time basis. Since I believe you won't let him go, we still may request his services from time to time.' Informal, but effective."

Tony grinned.

"He doesn't waste words."

"Why do you want this job, Tony?"

"I fell in love with this place.   I want to make my home here.   I like what I do now. But I prefer law enforcement work. I'd eventually like to take more classes in that field."

"A stepping stone to an FBI job?"

"No, sir. That's a nice change of pace. But I missed my wife and son when I traveled. Hopping around the country full time isn't for me."

"The job is yours."

"Just like that?"

"You're my last interview. The others had no more experience and not in this park. You can step right into the year round position with no training. That's a very compelling argument, even without these recommendations."

"Thank you, sir."

"And congratulations on your recent marriage. Go tell your wife."

"Thank you, sir."

He left the building, flashing a grin at Don on the way out. Don reclaimed his office.

"Well, Don, you got your way."

"There was no contest, was there?"

"No. That one's a lifer."

"He'll probably end up with my job."

"I'm shocked that you think anyone's good enough."

"That one is. Just had to get him to give up the idea of being a preacher. Been trying for two years. I think having a family did what I couldn't."

"The FBI may try to steal him away."

"Let 'em try. I'll just turn him loose once in a while, if they want him. But he don't want to be running all over the country. I'm not worried about losing him."

"That's what he said, but I'm glad you agree. I'd hate to think this is a short term appointment."

***

Tony dug through one of the boxes stacked in the corner of the livingroom. They had packed everything from his apartment, intending to unpack it only when they moved into ranger housing in September. But he needed something to occupy his mind.

After three weeks of 'can't wait for Brett to go to bed' fun, they had been forced to take a break. For the third night Kelly had told him that there would be no sex. He had thought himself prepared for this inevitable event. *Wrong!* The first night he had discovered that he had to stay out of the bedroom until he could not keep his eyes open. Tonight he found it impossible to concentrate on the television. Maybe thinking about the national park killer would distract him.

He pulled out the file with everything he had collected from the internet, newspapers, and working with the FBI. He made notes on a legal pad.

The unsub began killing about twelve years ago on the east coast.

Then, almost eight years ago, he moved his hunting ground west.

During the transitional phase, he killed the only two times I know of outside a national park– the Cumberland Mountains of Tennessee and the Missouri Ozarks. Except for the two FBI agents.

Because he's killed all over the country, he must travel for a living. But not a truck driver. A truck would be too noticeable. Let's say a traveling salesman. Business people fly and there aren't many major airports near national parks.

Tony leaned back. This accomplished nothing, but kept his mind off sex. He continued.

He hunts the parks because that's where it's easiest to find rich hikers. He's studied topographic maps. He knows the trails. Looks for rich, macho types. He wants them alone.

Does he rob them for the money, or just for the souvenirs? For the money. Garret said he only left valuables that contained a GPS.

But the real thrill is the hunt. Almost all the wounds are from behind. He probably tells them they can go, then wings them. Doesn't give them much of a chance. Doesn't want to take the chance that one will get away. Maybe one almost did.

He picked up a report from the FBI.

He hunts with a .222. Light, with little kick. And he uses a silencer. Doesn't want to attract attention. He's real good at avoiding attention.

Physically, he's a big man. Big arms. Strong.

Tony felt a chill as sweat began rolling off his body. The papers rattled in his hand. His breath came in gasps and his heart raced.

Am I having a heart attack?

Then he recognized the symptoms. Not a heart attack, but a panic attack. He worked to calm himself, using prayer in addition to the more common relaxation techniques. When the episode passed, he felt exhausted.

What caused that? He might not have chosen the best activity for a late night distraction. Fatigue made him more vulnerable. No need for panic. FBI agents watched the apartment round the clock. He gathered the papers and slipped them into the top box. *Guess I'm tired enough to sleep.*

***

"You had some awful nightmares," Kelly said the next morning.

"Tell me about it." Tony rubbed his face. "I made the mistake of studying my killer files last night."

"Why would you do that?"

"I needed something to take my mind off you."

"Just one more night. Then we can have fun again. I don't like this any more than you do. You're pretty wild in bed for a former seminary student."

He grinned.

"Making up for lost time. I should be able to sleep tonight, even laying beside you. I'm beat. This morning I need to drop off a book I borrowed from Betty."

"Go ahead. I'll take Brett to the sitter and meet you at work."

"Okay. Love you."

"I love you."

They kissed and he walked to Gil and Betty's house. She met him on the deck.

"Here's your book, Betty. Thanks."

"Don't mention it. How are you this morning?"

"Tired. Where's Gil off to today?"

"Oh, he's just in the garage."

"Morning, Tony."

"Hi, Gil." Tony felt a chill and his chest tightened. He had a sudden urge to run. "Better get to work. See you both later."

He had to force himself to walk, battling a rising panic. *What's going on? This makes no sense.* The closer he came to park headquarters, the more his panic dissipated. When he entered the building, he let his breath out. Don noticed.

"You're white as a sheet. What's going on?"

"I don't know. I had a panic attack last night. Then nightmares. And another one this morning. Last night I thought it was from studying my file on the killer. But that doesn't explain this morning."

"Maybe all this is just getting to you."

"Maybe."

Kelly walked in and he had to explain his appearance to her too. She hugged him, but asked no questions. He felt relieved, because he had no answers.

The day passed in a fog. That night, Tony beat Brett to bed.

He woke just after three, sitting up, sweat pouring off him, his heart pounding. This time he remembered the nightmare. He ran from the killer and woke only when he was shot. He padded from the bedroom, not wanting to wake Kelly. After a glass of water, he finally quit shaking.

Tony paced around the apartment, trying to understand why this fear had materialized. *It started with that file. At Glacier I got scared, but didn't know why until they hypnotized me. Reading that stuff last night, I must have figured out something. But what?*

He stared at the stack of boxes for minutes before approaching. Still, it took some time for him to pull out the file. Removing the legal pad, he studied his notes. He decided to concentrate on his description of the killer.

Big, strong man. Traveling salesman.

"Gil," Tony whispered, as he began sweating and shaking again.

He fought the tremors and rising panic. *Am I being paranoid? Gil's never been anything but nice to me. Never shown any sign of violence or even meanness.*

He paced, trying to calm himself, trying to talk himself out of his suspicion. *He's a big, traveling salesman. You need more evidence than that to accuse someone of being a serial killer.*

Tony braked. *He framed me.* It seemed obvious. Who had more opportunity and access? Gil had hidden the rifle behind the house after planting Tony's hair on it. He had plenty of excuses to enter Tony's apartment to collect the hair. And he could easily have found the antler off Tony's key ring, either outside or in the apartment. That may have given him the idea to frame his tenant.

Gil and Betty moved to Spruce Lake eight years ago. But where was it they came from? Iowa? No. Ohio. Just about the time the killings shifted from east to west.

Tony ran his hands through his hair, remembering his encounter with Gil after returning from Glacier. He sank into a chair when his knees felt rubbery.

Gil saw me at Glacier. He was waiting on the deck to ambush me. He uses a silencer. Tony's stomach churned. *My big mouth probably saved my life. I'm still alive because Gil knows I can't identify him.*

I'm not paranoid. Gil is a serial killer. I need to tell the FBI so they can prove it.

He pulled on a sweatshirt and slipped into the cool mountain air. With the nearest street light a half block away and no lighted windows in the neighborhood, he felt certain that he could cross the street undetected. In the star light he found the stairs leading to the loft above the garage. He did not have to knock. An FBI agent opened the door.

"Get in here. What do you think you're doing?"

Tony entered the darkened observation post.

"There's no one around to see me. This couldn't wait."

"Did you get a threat?"

"No. But you need to check out Gil Simon."

"Your former landlord?"

"Yeah. He's a traveling salesman. And he was on the road at the time of the murder in Glacier. He was gone when the hiker was killed here. You can check some of the other dates."

"Okay. We'll follow up on that. Now go home before someone sees you." Tony nodded and looked outside before descending the stairs. The agent shook his head. "Amateurs. He's seeing killers behind every bush."

***

Tony's nightmares did not completely abate, but subsided to a manageable number. He told no one else, not wanting them to act differently around Gil. For his part, he avoided Gil for fear that he would do the same. The sight of his long-time friend raised the hair on the back of his neck. He rehearsed relaxed encounters, topics of conversation, hoping that if he could not avoid Gil, he could hide his fear.

"Tony!" He leaped sideways, spinning to face Don. "Good grief, reverend! You're jumpier than a cat in a kennel. I hope they catch this guy soon. You're a wreck."

Tony let his breath out.

"I know. I want him caught more than anybody."

"Labor Day weekend's coming. You'll be too busy to be nervous."

"I hope so."

"Kevin says he's all packed. Tuesday's his last day. His family will be here with a moving van on Wednesday. With any luck, you and Kelly can move next weekend."

"We've been packing. Brett's excited about moving. Thinks it will be great living next to you."

"I'm looking forward to that myself. How's he feel about starting school?"

"He's excited about that too."

"He's just happy about everything. Here. Take these fliers to the sheriff's office."

Tony glanced at the sheets warning hikers against going out alone and describing the serial killer's preferred victims. He felt a chill.

"Not taking any chances."

"The park service is posting them all over the country this weekend. I have Kelly and Red putting them up now. But Ryan can put them around town too."

"Good idea."

"Glad you approve. Now get to work."

"Yes, sir."

"Oh, get lost."

Tony drove to the court house and handed the fliers to a deputy. As he returned to his pickup, Gil waved to him from two doors down. Tony took a deep breath and forced a smile. When Gil approached, he chose a stance that he hoped would hide his nerves. Leaning against the pickup, he hooked his free hand in his back pocket. That should hide any trembling and present a non-defensive stance. He focused on Gil's mouth to avoid looking him in the eye.

"Morning, Gil. What you up to today?"

"Delivering key rings to the gift shop. How bout yourself?"

"Delivering too. Fliers to the cops. Got plans for the big weekend?"

Gil snorted.

"Yeah. Work. I have to leave Saturday night."

Tony felt a chill. *Another hunting trip.* He only hesitated a few seconds.

"Where to this time?"

"Texas."

"Oh, that's a long one."

"Too long. We never see you since you moved."

Tony managed a grin.

"I'm really enjoying married life. Don't get out much."

"I'll bet you are. Let me know when you get your new house. I'll be glad to help you with the move."

"Thanks, Gil. I'd better get back to work. Lots to do before this weekend."

"Have a good one."

Tony climbed into the pickup, put it in reverse, and nearly backed into a car. He gave Gil a shrug and a sheepish grin before checking behind him and backing out. *So much for looking relaxed and casual. At least I can relax when he leaves town, even if that means he's off killing someone else.*

***

Sunday morning Tony felt much better. Gil's absence had meant a good night's sleep for him. When he and Kelly entered park headquarters, they heard Don cursing.

"That can't be good," Kelly said.

"There you are," Don said. "Blasted FBI. They take months to follow up on a lead, then decide they have to do it Labor Day weekend. Evidently a hiker saw a big man wearing camouflage breaking down a rifle near the Aspen Vista way back when."

"That is slow."

"They gave some lame excuse that the witness didn't report it right away and it took them a long time to sort through all the other tips. Who cares! I tried to convince them to wait till Tuesday. What difference will two days make when the trail's this cold? But they wouldn't hear of it. They're flying up by helicopter. Won't be there for a couple hours. Tony, will you ride up there and meet them? I can't spare anyone to go with you this weekend."

"I understand."

"Put on a GPS so we know where to find you."

"There's already one on the saddle."

"I know. Just humor me."

"Okay." He kissed Kelly. "I'll see you this evening."

"Be careful."

"Yes, ma'am."

"If you get there before they do," Don said. "Start looking by the tree growing out of the split rock. The hiker remembered that."

"Okay."

***

Tony enjoyed getting away from the holiday weekend crowds. He saw a few hikers on the lower part of the trail, but by the time he reached the choke in Elk Creek he had left them behind. He arrived at Aspen Vista an hour and a half after leaving park headquarters. Before dismounting, he enjoyed the view. The trail overlooked a valley thick with Quaking Aspen, the leaves already turning their fall gold.

He hobbled his horse near the tree line but away from the split rock. With no room for a helicopter to land, he did not have to worry about the FBI spooking his mount. He approached the rock, keeping his eyes on the ground. During the ride, he had convinced himself of the futility of this endeavor. *But who knows. We might find the clue that cracks the case.*

Tony's back hit the ground in tall grass. He gasped, trying desperately to catch his breath. An incident from his teens flashed through his mind. He had been hit in the chest by a friend's wild fast ball. This hurt worse.

Oh, God! I've been shot!

He looked at his chest. No blood. The vest had saved his life. But Gil would come to finish the job. Rising to his hands and knees, Tony crawled into thicker cover as fast as he could with the wind knocked out of him.

I can't get back to my horse. I'd be a sitting duck. I can outrun Gil once I can breath. I just have to stay ahead of him until then.

He stopped in dense cover, trying to breath quietly. He heard Gil back at the rock.

"Damn it, Tony! I never thought they'd put a vest on you! I didn't want you to suffer! You're a nice guy, not like the rest of 'em! Come out now and I'll get this over quick!"

Not a chance, Gil!

Tony rose to a crouch and eased through the undergrowth until it thinned. Then he ran, heading in the general direction of the ranger station.

Stay under cover. Don't give him a clear shot. When his breath came harder, he became aware of pain in his chest. *Cracked rib.* He did his best to ignore it.

He skirted a clearing. *Don't give Gil a clear shot. Make this as hard for him as you can.* He hoped that this forced run would reduce Gil's accuracy. He had little experience keeping up with an uninjured quarry.

The shot spun him around, throwing him down a slope into buck brush. This time blood soaked his left arm. Adrenaline kept him from feeling the wound to his triceps. But the arm proved useless when he crawled away. Again in thicker cover, he stood and ran.

When he stopped to rest, he could hear Elk Creek. He glanced at the arm. *I'm losing a lot of blood, but I can't take the time to stop it. I have to keep going!*

"Tony, you're leaving a blood trail a kid could follow! Why put yourself through this? You know how good I am! Give it up!"

Never! You may kill me, but not because I surrendered!

Tony ran again, staying off the trail, but following Elk Creek. He remembered another time in his life when he had felt this tired, during a Wisconsin flood.

God, help me. Don't let him win.

He saw a tree splinter just ahead of him, and dodged to his left, closer to the creek. The roar of the water drowned out any sounds now. Gil could not hear his labored breathing when he stopped to rest. He could outrun Gil at his best. But not with blood flowing from his arm at an alarming rate. He could not run much farther.

I don't have to. It would be suicide to jump into Elk Creek above the Choke. But if he could make it past there, the jump would be merely crazy. *I swam in that kind of current before. But with two arms.* Only a completely desperate man would attempt to swim Elk Creek with one good arm.

Tony ran, zigzagging. Again, a tree splintered. He saw the water spouting in the air as it forced its way between the rocks. He would have thirty feet of open rock to cross before he reached the precipice. At the edge of the trees he dodged to the right, hoping Gil would think he had made the sane decision to stay on the trail. Tony changed direction and leaped as far from the rocks as he could, praying to God to help him clear the undertow.

Gil ran to the edge of the rocks, cursing. He pointed his silencer-equipped rifle at the pool below, waiting for Tony to surface. Nothing. He searched the edges of the pool. No sign of Tony. The water had probably done his job for him. But he would take no chances. He followed the trail, searching the creek for his prey.

***

"Don," Kelly said. "When's Tony supposed to get back?"

"They didn't say. I'll go ask the yahoos in the van out there."

"They won't like that."

Don laughed.

"I know."

He walked across the street and knocked on the back door of the surveillance van. The agent Tony had told about Gil opened the door, scowling.

"You're going to blow our cover."

"Who cares. When will Tony be back from your wild goose chase?"

"We didn't send him anywhere."

"Not you specifically. Someone from the FBI wanted him to meet your helicopter at Aspen Vista."

"They never tell us anything. I'll check."

He used his cell phone and asked for Garret. He frowned when they connected him. He relayed Don's question, then had to explain further. Don felt ill when he saw the agent's expression. He handed the phone to Don and took the other agent's phone. Don spoke first.

"My God, you didn't send him up there."

"No," Garret said. "Was he wearing the Kevlar?"

"Yes. And I made him put on a GPS."

"Was anyone with him?"

"No. We're too busy. The bastard knew I couldn't spare anyone this weekend."

"He's patient. Give those agents the frequency of the GPS. Our chopper will join the sheriff's just as soon as we can get there. Don't give up. Tony's resourceful."

Don disconnected and trudged back to the office where Kelly waited on the front step. She put her hands to her mouth and shook her head.

"We don't know anything, Kelly. Tony's smart and he's wearing that vest."

"It was a trap."

"I'm sorry. I should have called back to make sure it was the FBI."

"No, Don. It's not your fault. What can we do?"

"Look up that GPS on the computer."

Kelly ran inside and brought up the program. The agents entered as the map came up.

"He's by Elk Creek! About a mile below the choke."

An agent called the information to the sheriff's office. Don had another idea.

"Look up the GPS from his saddle."

Kelly did and her face drained of color.

"Aspen Vista."

Don squeezed her shoulder.

"Better the horse there than Tony. He got away, Kelly."

She forced a smile.

"Yeah. He got away."

She brought up Tony's GPS again. It had not moved. They heard a helicopter fly over. Don used the radio to call in all rangers to organize a ground search, then switched to the sheriff's frequency. They listened to Ryan talking with the helicopter and his deputies.

"We're right over the coordinates, but there's no sign of Tony. I'll let Tim and Wade off so they can do a ground search."

Minutes dragged by. Kelly pointed at the computer screen.

"Look! It's moving!"

Don smiled, but the next moment the radio dashed their hopes.

"We found the GPS in the creek. We'll work our way downstream."

Ryan told them he would send additional personnel. Kelly pushed her chair back and ran to the sleeping room. Don sighed.

"What am I supposed to tell her?"

"We haven't found a body," the agent said.

"That's a real comfort." Don found Kelly sobbing. He patted her back. "Don't give up. Pray. I have."

"You?"

"Even me. The reverend's got friends in real high places. Don't forget that."

"Thanks, Don. What do I tell Brett?"

"Keep him in the dark for now. You told him you might have to work late. We'll tell Cindy that she needs to keep him overnight. We'll just say that you have to work real late."

"I don't know if I can pull that off, Don."

"I'll help you. And I'll call Lois to come sit with you."

"I want to go look for Tony."

"No."

"I need to, Don."

"No. You need to stay here for your son. I don't want you out there too."

Kelly finally nodded.

***

During the next hour the sheriff's helicopter ferried rangers and deputies to locations along Elk Creek. At the ranger station, they heard the FBI pilot report that he had left Garret and another agent at the creek and would take others to Aspen Vista to investigate.

Garret sought out Ryan, who had joined the search.

"Sheriff, what can you tell me?"

"We've found nothing but the GPS. Even after being in the water, you can see blood on the band."

"Hellfire! I told him he was safe."

"Nobody counted on this. Let's go. We're not finding him standing here."

They worked their way down the creek, searching the rocky banks and the stream bed.

"How cold's this water?"

"Cold enough to cause hypothermia in a matter of minutes."

They looked under every log, behind every boulder in the creek, which had widened and slowed. When a tree hung over the water, they inspected under its branches. An hour passed. The only traffic on Ryan's radio reported nothing found.

"Sheriff!" Garret shouted, pointing. He ran across the thigh-deep water to the spot on the far bank where feet emerged from beneath evergreen branches. "Tony!"

Tony lay face down. Garret pulled him out, noticing the wound on his arm and his complete lack of color. He felt Tony's neck and looked up as Ryan arrived.

"I've got a pulse. Weak."

Ryan called on the radio while removing his backpack.

"We need that chopper and medic **now**!"

"The wound's just oozing."

"The cold may have stopped the bleeding. We need to warm him as fast as we can. Cut his clothes off. I have a blanket, but he has no body heat to hold in. We'll use ours and the blanket until the medic gets here. I'll bandage the wound while you're working on the clothes."

Garret found the other bullet hole in Tony's shirt.

"He'd be dead without the vest."

"He still may be."

"Nothing negative! You're going to make it, Tony. Don't give up. Remember Kelly and Brett."

Soon after they lay with Tony between them, deputies arrived. They rolled Tony to put a blanket under him, then added more on top and wrapped his head in a sweatshirt.

Twenty minutes later the helicopter and paramedic hovered overhead. A winch lowered him and a litter filled with warm blankets. They only paused long enough to wrap Tony in the blankets, before lifting him to the helicopter.

Garret examined the holes in Tony's shirt and the damage to the vest.

Then he called his helicopter to take him to the crime scene.

***

At park headquarters, listening to the radio traffic, they heard about Tony's gunshot wounds and hypothermia. Then the pilot reported their destination, the nearest hospital. Don told Kelly and Lois that he would drive. He made the half-hour trip in twenty minutes.

It seemed that the entire staff of the small hospital had been called in for this one patient. Lois pointed out three doctors. A nurse showed them to a waiting room. Every few minutes Don found someone who told him that they knew nothing yet. One hundred minutes after they arrived, a balding doctor came to the waiting room.

"Mrs. Wagner?"

"How is he?"

"Alive. Stable, but critical. We're raising his body temperature, but he is still dangerously hypothermic. He lost a lot of blood. We're replacing that."

"Can I see him?"

"Not yet. Someone will come get you."

"Are his wounds life threatening?"

"No. He has muscle damage and a fracture of his left humerus and a fractured rib. He aspirated some water. But, if he can recover from the hypothermia, his body will heal."

He left and they waited. Pastor Johnson arrived and they prayed together. When Don returned from his next excursion, he had a new report.

"There's two FBI agents guarding the emergency room."

"Tony's the only living person who's seen the killer," Kelly said.

"When he wakes, he'll tell everyone."

***

Garret's eyebrows met and he lost his temper.

"He what!"

The agent swallowed and repeated it.

"Wagner came to me a few nights ago, all shook up."

"What did he tell you?"

"He said we should check out his former landlord."

"And why am I only hearing about this now?"

"I figured the pressure was getting to him."

"You idiot! Did you do anything to follow up on it?"

"I checked. This Gil Simon is on a business trip."

"Someone get me an open search warrant for all of Simon's property. I want everything. Get a description of him and put it out. Armed and extremely dangerous. Bring his wife in for questioning." He glared at the agent. "You're suspended. And God help you if Tony dies."

***

Like the rest of Spruce Lake's residents, Betty had noticed the sudden flurry of activity and the return of the FBI agents. She had called all of her friends and finally learned that someone had been flown to the hospital with gunshot wounds. She prayed for the victim and hoped it was no one she knew.

She stayed up late, trying to learn more. She had just decided to give up and go to bed when someone pounded on the door. She looked at the clock. Eleven.

"Who could that be?" She turned on the outside light and saw the grim FBI agents. "Has something happened to Tony?"

"Why would you say that, ma'am?"

"He's a dear friend. Why else would you come here?"

"Ma'am, come with us. Our senior agent will fill you in."

"Of course. I'll just grab my sweater."

Now Betty sat in Don's office while the rest of the ranger station swarmed with FBI agents. She kept looking for Tony, or Kelly, or Don. Her worry deepened by the minute. She recognized Agent Garret when he entered and closed the door.

"Sir, has something happened to Tony?"

"What makes you think that, ma'am?"

"I just can't think of any other reason why you'd want to talk to me."

"We wanted you out of the way so we could search your house."

"My house? Why?"

"Because we believe that your husband is the national park killer." Betty's jaw dropped. She could only stare. "And today he shot Tony Wagner."

"That's ridiculous. We love Tony like a son. Gil would never hurt him. This is insane." She stopped. "Is Tony . . . dead?"

"No. But he's in critical condition."

"Please, Lord. Not Tony."

"Your husband shot him."

"No. Why would you think that?"

"Because Tony told us."

The color left her face as tears came.

"Tony wouldn't lie. How could I live with a killer for twenty years and not know it? What can I do to help you catch him?"

Now Garret stared.

"Tony's word is enough to convince you, ma'am?"

"Tony has never lied to me. I can't say the same for Gil. I explained it away as one night stands when he was on the road. I convinced myself it didn't matter because we had a good marriage when he was here. But he's been killing people. What if I had confronted him?"

"He probably would have admitted to fooling around. He only killed strangers."

"But Tony."

"We think he figured out that Tony suspected him. Tell me everything you can think of that made you suspicious."

"The expensive watch he wears. He said it was a gift from his employer, but I thought they would have engraved the back of it."

"How long has he had it?"

"I'm not sure. Since before we moved here."

"What else?"

"A key that doesn't fit any of our locks. A receipt from a gas station in Cody, Wyoming when he was supposed to be in Nebraska. A parking ticket from Cheyenne, Wyoming when he was supposed to be in Arizona."

"Do you remember when you found those?"

"The key's been there for years. I probably noticed it six years ago. The last time I checked, it was still there. The receipt was last fall, September, I think. The ticket, about two years ago."

"Can you pinpoint it any closer than that?"

"Spring. Maybe April."

"Anything else, ma'am?"

"Not that I can think of. But if I remember anything else, I'll tell you."

"How often does your husband contact you when he's on the road?"

"Every morning."

"We'll have your phone tapped before then."

"I can't talk to him. He'll know I know."

"No, he won't. Tony's been shot. You're very upset. He'll think that's what's going on. When he calls in the morning, you'll tell him Tony's dead. You'll ask him to come home. Where's he claim to be this time?"

"Texas. But he always calls on his cell phone. Can you tell where he is?"

"If you keep him talking long enough. Unless he has a real old phone without a GPS. Even then, we can pin down the tower he's transmitting from. Since we know he's in the area, it will give us a better idea where to search. Hopefully, if he thinks Tony's dead, he'll feel safe enough to come home."

"Will I have to see him?"

"No. We'll grab him before he gets to your door."

"Good. I don't think I can hide my revulsion."

***

"Mrs. Wagner."

Kelly opened her eyes to see the doctor standing over her.

"Is he better?"

"His temperature is normal. He's still in a coma. But you can see him."

She sat up.

"What time is it?"

"Seven AM."

She followed him to the intensive care unit. When she saw Tony, she put her hand to her chest.

"He's so pale."

"It's an improvement over last night."

She held his right hand. Bandages and an air splint encased his left arm. An oxygen mask covered his nose and mouth, so she kissed his forehead.

"When will he come out of the coma?"

"We don't know. When his body says he's well enough. He's had a very traumatic experience. He needs to rest. This is the best way."

"Is he out of danger?"

"Immediate danger. Because of the aspiration, he is at risk for pneumonia. That's why we've elevated his head and are keeping him on oxygen. I suggest that you go see your son."

"I don't want to leave. But you're right. I need to tell Brett about this. How do I tell a five-year-old that his daddy's been shot?"

"You don't. Tell him he's been hurt. Tell him what happens when you fall into cold water. Don't tell him that someone tried to kill his father."

"You're right. Thanks, doctor. I'd like to stay with Tony a while longer."

"Stay as long as you like. When you come back, you can be with him most of the time."

***

Brett hugged Kelly when she reached Cindy's house.

"I missed you, Mommy. Where's Daddy?"

"Let's walk home and get you some clean clothes."

"Okay. Is Daddy still working?"

"Your daddy had an accident. He'll be fine, but he's in the hospital."

"What happened?"

"He fell in the creek."

"Did he drown?"

"No. You know how cold the water in the creek is."

"Yeah."

"If you're in cold water too long, you can't warm yourself up, no matter how many blankets you put on. They have to put you in the hospital to make you warm."

"How?"

"I'm not sure. But they can do all kinds of things you can't do at home."

"How long will it take to warm him up?"

"A few days. He isn't just cold. He broke his arm and a rib too."

"When he fell?"

"It happened at the same time."

"Does it hurt?"

"He's sleeping now, so it doesn't hurt too bad."

"Can I see him?"

"Not yet, honey. They don't let kids visit. I'll bet he'd like it if you drew him a picture."

"Yeah!"

"In a couple days, you can talk to him on the phone."

"Can't I now?"

"The doctor won't let him. They won't even put a phone in his room."

"What about his cell phone?"

"They make you turn those off in a hospital."

"Oh."

"I'm going to take a shower while you color your picture. Then I'll have to go back to the hospital."

"They let you stay with Daddy?"

"Yes."

"Good. He needs you to take care of him when he's sick."

***

Betty waited with Garret, Dimaggio and Ferguson for Gil's call. As she expected, the phone rang at eight o'clock. She picked it up while they listened.

"Hello."

"Hi, Betty. What's up?"

"Oh, Gil. It's just awful. Tony's dead. Someone shot him."

"What? Are you sure?"

"Yes. No one can believe it. Poor Kelly. Oh, Gil, can you come right home?"

"Yeah. Of course. Why didn't you call me?"

"It was so late when I heard. I knew you'd have your phone shut off. Who would hurt that dear boy? He didn't have an enemy in the world."

"I don't know, honey. I don't know. I'm down near Austin. It'll take me a while to get there. But I'll start back right now. I suppose the FBI is around."

"Oh, they're everywhere."

"They been asking you any questions?"

Betty hesitated.

"Me? They have better things to do than talk to me."

"Suppose so. I'll call again in the morning. Better get packed."

"Okay."

"Bye now."

"Goodbye, Gil."

She disconnected and Garret looked at Ferguson. He reported.

"I didn't get the exact tower, but somewhere in the Four Corners area."

"He's headed for Mexico. Alert law enforcement in that area."

"But won't he come back," Betty said. "Now that he thinks Tony's dead?"

"We hope so. But he claims to be near Austin. He's buying himself time to confirm that Tony's dead. We have the hospital sealed up. We'll tell the media that he's dead."

"What about Tony's parents?"

"They've been contacted. We'll keep them informed."

"How is Tony?"

"Improved, but still in a coma. Agent Ferguson will stay with you and monitor all your calls. Stay off the phone in case your husband calls. Tell people you're too upset to talk."

"Okay. And if Gil calls back before tomorrow?"

"Act surprised. Ask if there's something wrong. Act heartbroken."

"That won't be an act."

***

Twenty-four hours after Tony arrived at the hospital, he opened his eyes, saw Kelly, smiled and squeezed her hand, then drifted off again. The following morning pain woke him. He groaned before he opened his eyes.

"Tony."

"Love you."

He removed the mask and smiled at her.

"I love you, Tony. How do you feel?"

"Not so good." He looked around. "What happened?"

"What do you remember?"

He licked his lips and frowned. "Thirsty." She offered him a glass with a straw. He spoke better after a drink. "I made it. Thank God."

She began to cry.

"Yes, thank God. Do you know who shot you?"

"Yeah."

"Who was it?"

"No. I'll tell Garret."

"There are FBI agents right outside."

"No. Just Garret. Tell them." She frowned, but quickly relayed the message, then returned with an agent following. "Get out!"

Kelly and the agent stared.

"Tony?"

"Get out!"

Kelly waved the agent out as Tony began coughing.

"What's wrong, Tony?"

"I'll tell Garret."

He coughed so hard that she summoned a nurse, who replaced the oxygen mask and raised the head of his bed higher. The coughing subsided. After she departed, Tony spoke through the mask.

"How bad am I hurt?"

"You have a broken rib and a broken humerus."

"Thank God for the bulletproof vest."

"For so many things."

The doctor entered and listened to his lungs. He ordered a chest x-ray.

"How are you feeling, Mr. Wagner?"

"Grateful to be alive."

"Other than that?"

"Wasn't too bad until that coughing fit."

"You aspirated water. Your lungs have some rattles. We'll treat you aggressively for pneumonia. I'll have the nurse switch your oxygen to a nasal cannula, but talk as little as possible."

"I'm tired anyhow."

"As soon as they finish the x-ray you can go back to sleep."

***

Garret arrived to find Tony sleeping again. Kelly took him to the waiting room.

"He said that he knows who shot him, but he would only tell you. When one of your agents came in, Tony snapped at him. I've never heard him like that."

"I don't blame him. He has good reason to be angry."

"Why? What happened?"

"I'm very sorry, Kelly. A few days ago, Tony told one of his surveillance detail the identity of the killer. That agent, who is now suspended, blew it off. Thought Tony was being paranoid."

"He knew days ago and he didn't say anything to me?"

"He followed the proper procedure. If the agent had done the same, we would have been tailing the suspect and this wouldn't have happened. I'm very sorry."

"At least you're not apologizing to his widow. Why couldn't he tell me?"

"He didn't tell anyone because he didn't want you to act differently toward the suspect."

"It's someone local?"

"Yes."

"That's why you want him to think Tony's dead?"

"Yes. Tony's the only one who can identify him. If he thinks he's tied up that loose end, he'll come back and we can grab him."

"Gil? It can't be Gil?"

"I'm afraid so. But don't share that with anyone."

"Oh, my God. Don't tell me Betty's involved."

"Doesn't seem to be. She's cooperating. She denied everything until

I told her that Tony suspected her husband. If he said so, it had to be true."

"He must have had an awful time hiding his suspicion from Gil. He must have failed."

"Simon is cautious. It wouldn't have taken much. It tears me up that we left him hanging in the wind when he thought we were backing him up."

"Apologize to him."

"I will. Why don't you get some rest. I'll stay with him until he wakes up."

"You don't have to do that."

"I'm staying till he wakes up anyhow."

"Okay. I'll catch a nap. Tell him I'm not far."

"I will."

Garret returned to Tony's room, selected a comfortable chair, and studied notes on his PDA. For the next hour, only the bubbling of the oxygen water bottle and Tony's occasional cough broke the silence.

"Kelly's a lot prettier to wake up to."

Garret dropped his PDA.

"But I bet you woke up faster when you saw my ugly face."

"Yeah."

He approached the bedside.

"I'm so sorry. The agent who blew you off is under suspension. I promise, no one in the Bureau will ever ignore you again."

"Thanks. He didn't tell anybody?"

"Not till you'd been airlifted to the hospital. Although, when you disappeared, he did check to see if Simon was in town."

"Have you caught him?"

"Not yet. His wife's cooperating. But when he called her this morning, he was closer to the Mexican border than he was yesterday. He isn't trusting the reports of your death."

"My death? My parents!"

Tony began coughing.

"Take it easy. We've kept them in the loop. I know there's a lot of other people who are pretty upset, but that can't be helped. Only a handful of people outside the Bureau know you're alive. Until he's caught, we'll try to keep it that way. How did you figure out that Simon was the killer?"

"Couldn't sleep. I went through your profile and it came to me that Gil fit. I couldn't talk myself out of it." Tony coughed. "And I realized that no one had a better opportunity to frame me. He had access to everything he planted. I just can't believe he thought it would stick."

"Maybe he framed you because he knew it wouldn't stick. He just wanted to distract us for a while."

"Huh. If he hadn't done that, I probably wouldn't have gotten interested in the case."

"And I wouldn't have involved you if we hadn't already cleared you. Framing you turned out to be his fatal mistake. Tell me what happened up there."

"Don told you about the call."

"Yeah."

"I started searching the ground. Hadn't been there long when he shot me in the chest. He didn't think I'd be wearing a vest." He coughed. "He said that he didn't want me to suffer. I wasn't like the others."

"He talked to you?"

"Yelled at me. I hid until I could breath. I ran, but I couldn't avoid him forever. After he wounded me, I couldn't stop the bleeding. Made me easy to track and I was getting weaker. My only chance . . ." Coughing interrupted him. When it subsided, Garret offered him water. "Thanks. I had to get below the Choke or I wouldn't survive Elk Creek. I jumped into the bowl. The last thing I remember was fighting to get to the surface."

"We found you quite a ways down stream. You'd crawled up on shore under some evergreen branches. You have *some* survival instincts."

"I understand you and Ryan saved my life."

"We just found you."

"They said you kept me warm until the helicopter arrived."

"Don't spread it around. Wouldn't want a lot of people to know that I was under a blanket with two other men."

Tony's laugh led to more coughing. After more water, his serious mood returned.

"Gil expected me to give up and die. Guess he really didn't know me. Do you have anything else on him?"

"Yes. Thanks to his wife. She remembered a parking ticket from Cheyenne, Wyoming and an extra key. We canvassed the area where the ticket was issued and the owner of a storage facility recognized him as Gilbert Peterson, a renter who's paid in cash for the past seven years. We found his car, a rifle, and what appear to be mementoes of his killings in the storage unit."

"So you don't know what he's driving?"

"We're working on that. Wyoming DMV did have a green Ford truck registered to a Gilbert Peterson and a drivers license for the same. The address given was the storage facility, with a post office box mailing address. We think he just used the PO box for Gilbert Peterson's bills."

"What if you don't catch him before I'm ready to get out of here?"

"You and your family will go into protective custody. You'll be in no shape to work for a while anyhow. Might as well take a vacation at government expense."

"Don won't like losing Kelly too."

"Don will do whatever it takes to protect you. And we'll make sure you have jobs to go back to."

"Okay."

Tony yawned.

"I'll let you rest. Contact me if you think of anything else. I've left instructions that you're to be put through, no matter what."

***

Tony did not need to stay in intensive care, but the FBI found it easier to conceal him there. His doctor wanted him to exercise to fight off the pneumonia. He walked around the unit, pushing his IV stand. By Saturday afternoon, the doctor informed him that he could go home, if the FBI approved.

Garret brought Kelly and Brett to the hospital. Tony hugged Brett with his good arm.

"I've missed you, son."

"I love you, Daddy. Are you feeling better?"

"A lot better."

"You broke your arm."

"And a rib."

"Does it hurt?"

"Not so much anymore."

Kelly kissed Tony.

"Brett, Mr. Garret needs to talk to your daddy for a while. Let's go for a walk."

When they left, Garret began.

"Tomorrow, your minister will tell the congregation that you're alive.

We'll also release Simon's name and picture to the media. Tonight, we're flying you to Fargo. You'll stay with your in-laws for a while, with protection."

"Why not my parents?"

"Because he had six years to find out everything he needed to know about your parents. With any luck, he won't think of looking for you in North Dakota. I don't think he'll even bother. He's too busy running. Have you ever been there? Flat as a table. We can see someone coming miles away."

"What a way to get to know my in-laws."

"You're a hero. What could be better?"

"I don't feel like a hero. I'd rather not leave Spruce Lake."

"I understand. But North Dakota will be safer for you and more manageable for us. Spruce Lake is a sniper's paradise. There's cover everywhere. Besides, do you really want to worry about Kelly working out in the park? Even if we send an agent with her, he can't protect her from a sniper."

"Do you think he'd go after Kelly or Brett?"

"To get to you, yes. Right now he doesn't know about the pile of evidence we're collecting. He thinks you're it." Tony nodded. "Don't get me wrong. We doubt he'll come after you. We're just not taking any chances."

"Thanks."

***

They arrived at the Thiel's Mapleton farm late that evening. John and Darlene welcomed them with hugs and tears. Darlene seemed reluctant to let go of Tony.

"We love you. Thank goodness you're okay."

"Thanks, Darlene. Thanks for keeping us."

"We're glad to have you as long as you need to stay."

"Thanks."

"You must be tired from your trip. I'll show you to your room."

He and Kelly left Brett with his grandparents and retired to the lower floor of the split level. He wrapped his good arm around her and they shared a long kiss. He sighed.

"I want to make love to you, but I'm just too tired."

"Tomorrow."

"Sounds good. Did you pack my condoms?"

"No. Let's make a baby."

He frowned.

"Maybe you shouldn't make that decision right now. You've had a lot of stress lately."

"Agreed. I won't deny that nearly losing you influenced my decision. But why not now? We have insurance. We want another baby. Brett's starting school. Why put it off?"

"Probably because I'm selfish. I like having you to myself at night. I like sex. I'm not looking forward to us being too tired for it."

She smiled.

"Well, that's honesty. And a compelling argument. When I had Brett, I had no love life."

"Think about it until tomorrow."

"Okay. I'll sleep on it."

***

Tony woke alone and disoriented. After sitting up, he recognized his surroundings. He made himself presentable before climbing the stairs. Darlene turned to greet him, but no words came from her open mouth.

"Weren't you expecting me?"

She blushed.

"Yes. I just wasn't expecting quite so much of you."

"Oh. Sorry. The way they have my arm hobbled to me, it's easier to skip the shirt. I can put one on if it bothers you."

"No. No. It's just, I didn't expect a seminary student to have a build like that."

He chuckled and took a seat at the kitchen island.

"Why, Darlene, you're not supposed to notice that."

"I'm not blind. Coffee?"

"Thanks."

"What would you like for breakfast?"

"Whatever's easiest for you."

"Cereal it is. Why isn't your arm in a cast?"

"A humerus fracture is hard to cast. Then there's the wound to treat. So I have to get by with this splint and hobble. Where's Kelly?"

"Giving Brett a tour of the barn. He's missed his animal friends."

"I'm sure he loves it here. But he needs to start kindergarten."

"We've made arrangements for him to start here on Monday. He's a couple weeks behind, but he knows most of that stuff already. You're right, he needs to get started. He'll know some of the kids in his class, so it won't be completely foreign to him."

"That's nice. I don't want him to fall behind. Is that your RV?"

"No. That monstrosity is FBI headquarters. They tell me that mast has cameras with 360 degree coverage of the surrounding area. Night vision and all that. Four agents. One will go to school with Brett. He'll stay outside. When you go anywhere, two will stay with you and one will keep an eye on the place."

"I think they're trying to make up for this."

He nodded toward his arm.

"Daddy!"

"Morning, Brett. You having fun?"

"Yeah! I miss Grandma and Grandpa."

"I know."

He patted Brett's head, then kissed Kelly.

"You look good this morning," she said.

"M-m. So do you."

She stood between his feet and rested her hands on his hips. A longer kiss followed. Darlene smiled.

"Brett, want to help me in my garden?"

"Sure, Grandma. Can I, Mommy?"

"Of course. I'll just help your daddy with his bandages." When Darlene and Brett left, she sighed. "Mom can read the signs."

Tony took her hand and they hurried to their bedroom.

"You still want to make a baby?"

"Yes."

She pulled off his sweat pants, then began undressing herself. He locked the door before drawing her to him. He kissed her lips, then her neck. She had become expert at keeping her voice down. She just moaned and backed toward the bed.

"Wait. I think I need to do this on my back for a while. Probably hurt less."

She caressed his thighs.

"Works for me. I don't want this to be unpleasant for you. Get comfortable."

Not an easy task, she helped him by positioning a pillow under his injured arm. Finally, he nodded and she joined him. She kept her hands off him, afraid she would hurt him more. But he did not need the extra stimulation. He finished with a grimace that stayed.

"Ow."

"What hurts?"

"Rib."

"Can I get you something?" He nodded and she retrieved his pain medication. "I'm sorry."

He forced a smile.

"Worth it."

***

"Hi, Don."

"Reverend! I didn't think the Feds would let you call."

"It's okay as long as I use my cell phone and don't tell you where I am."

"How you doing?"

"Going stir crazy. I can walk, but not much else."

"Thought with your paid vacation, you newlyweds wouldn't get out of bed."

"Busted rib. Once a day's about all I can handle."

"That stinks."

"Tell me about it. What's going on there?"

"After everybody found out you're alive and that Gil's the killer, we had a town meeting. Garret attended. People are up in arms. And pretty scared. No one knows where they took Betty either. Her house is locked up tight. Probably just as well. Even though Garret told everybody she isn't involved and she's cooperating, some people were looking for anyone to blame."

"That's too bad. I feel sorry for her. And I'm sorry we're leaving you short-handed."

"Don't worry about it. Kevin talked to his father-in-law. He's staying on till the end of the month."

"Oh. I don't feel quite so bad."

"No sign of Gil yet."

"I hope they catch him soon. I want to come home."

"By the time you do, you'll have a home to move into. Kevin's stuff's all gone. He already had the truck rented. A bunch of us are moving your stuff this weekend. You may not be able to find anything when Lois puts it away, but it'll be there."

"That's awfully nice. Thank everyone for us."

"I'll do that. You know Garret really talked you up at that meeting. He flat out told everybody that you figured out that Gil was the killer before the FBI did."

"That was nice of him."

"Afterward, he suggested that you take some more classes so you're qualified to investigate felonies. Maybe you'd like to do that while you're healing up."

"Maybe. I'll do some checking. If I could find something on line, it wouldn't matter that I'm in . . . where I am."

"Uh-huh. You almost gave it away, didn't you."

"I still have a big mouth."

"Maybe they'll teach you to keep it shut."

"I'd better go before I get in trouble. Hope to see you soon."

***

"We got him," Garret said without fanfare.

Tony nearly dropped the phone.

"Where?"

"Trying to cross the border at Laredo. Not where we expected him. I'm flying down there to question him myself."

"Did he resist arrest?"

"Once he saw he was surrounded and outnumbered he surrendered without a fight."

"Thank God. We can go home."

"Yeah."

"How soon? I like my in-laws, but after three weeks, I'm ready for my own bed."

"The agents will put you on a commercial flight in the morning. Other agents will meet you at the airport and take you home."

"Sounds good to me. Any chance I can find out what he has to say?"

"About you?"

"Yeah."

"I'll bring you a tape. You cracked this case for us. I've recommended you for a citation."

"I just connected the dots. You collected them first."

"That's how you solve crimes. You had the advantage of knowing Simon. But you still have potential as an investigator."

"Thanks. When no one was trying to kill me, I enjoyed it."

"If you took additional classes, I could get you on retainer as a consultant."

"No kidding?"

"Serious as a heart attack. It wouldn't be much of a retainer. And don't think it's a bribe to keep you from suing the Bureau."

"Suing? I don't blame the FBI for one man's mistake. Unless he gets a big promotion."

"He's on suspension, pending termination. Even if he hadn't endangered your life, he ignored a source giving him the identity of a serial killer. We follow up all leads, even anonymous tips. He blew off someone close to the case. That's inexcusable."

"I forgive him. But I wouldn't want to work with him again either."

"I understand you have a long recovery ahead of you."

"Yeah. I had a checkup a couple days ago. The arm's healing good, but it'll still be a few weeks before I can go back to work. The rib's better, so I'm not so bored."

"What's that have to do with boredom?" When Tony just chuckled, Garret laughed. "Enjoying Kelly's company, are you?"

"Yeah."

"Good. You know you're in line for a reward too."

"A reward. I wouldn't think, as a federal employee, that I'd be eligible."

"I'll see that you get it, even if it has to go toward a trust fund for your kid."

"That would be great. He needs a college fund."

"If you find the time, think about those classes. I'll mail you a list of what's available in Denver. As soon as we get charges filed against Simon, I'll come see you."

"What charge are you using to hold him?"

"Attempted murder. You're the reason he can't kill anyone else."

***

Tony settled into a routine of walking Brett to and from school, cooking, cleaning, and rehabilitating. He registered for a week-long forensics class, though he hated the thought of missing Kelly and Brett that long. He and Kelly had failed to make a baby, but not for lack of trying.

She often worked with far less than eight hours sleep. And he made her lunch every day, so she could come home for recreation. She began to look forward to his class.

Everyone in town asked him about his health and his experiences. He finally consented to an interview with the local paper, which stopped many of the questions about the latter.

With his left upper arm still hobbled to his side, but his forearm free, Tony raked leaves while Lois, now his neighbor, bagged them into pumpkin leaf bags.

"That should be enough, Tony. With all these evergreens, it's hard to fill my pumpkins."

"Glad I could help. We'll be seeing snow before long."

"Then the cross country skiers will descend on us. How do you feel about your first winter here?"

"Looking forward to it. It's nice to be outside instead of in a classroom."

"But you'll be in a classroom next week."

"Only for a week. That won't be bad. Hopefully, the doctor will clear me to go back to work after that. But I'll be behind a desk for a while."

"Looks like you have a visitor."

Tony recognized the driver when the car came to a stop. He waved to Garret. After exchanging pleasantries with Lois, the agent held up a tape.

"I promised you this." He followed Tony inside and surveyed the house. "Not bad."

"We like it. Coffee?"

"Yeah. I'll pour. Just stick that in. I only included the parts you need to see."

Tony sank to his favorite chair, and soon Gil appeared on the screen, dressed in orange prison coveralls, looking relaxed. Off screen, Garret asked a question.

"You know that your wife is cooperating with us?"

"Don't surprise me. I tried to kill Tony. She'll never forgive me for that. He was like a son to us."

"But you tried to frame him."

Gil laughed.

"I knew that'd slide off him like water off a duck. He was going to church on Sunday, then someone always asks him to dinner afterward. He never gets home till two, three o'clock. And Betty sees him come. He usually stops up to visit after he changes clothes. I wouldn't of framed him if I didn't know he'd have an alibi."

"So why'd you try to kill him?"

Gil smiled sadly.

"He'd figured me out. The boy's too smart for his own good. I don't feel a bit of regret about the others, but the thought of killing Tony brought me to tears. He didn't deserve to die, like they did. But he knew, so I didn't have a choice. I didn't want him to suffer though. I was real careful. Lined up a good kill shot so he'd never know what hit him. And damned if he wasn't wearing a vest. Never thought you'd put a vest on him."

"We did a few things you never thought of."

"Guess so. Bout scared the life out of me when I saw him up in Montana. He looked right at me. I was sure the gig was up, especially when those two came after me. I got out of there fast as I could on the back roads, then laid low listening to the radio. Heard the description of my truck a dozen times. Couldn't figure out why they weren't talking about me. I was plenty shook up. Torched the truck and hiked into Cody, then caught the bus to Cheyenne. I was still plenty cautious when I came home."

Gil drank from a coffee cup before continuing.

"I still thought Tony'd remember, once he saw me again. I heard him come home that morning. Took my Smith & Wesson with the silencer out on the deck and waited for him."

Tony shuddered.

"He was jumpy, but all he could talk about was getting married. I relaxed a little and managed to coax him into saying he hadn't seen me. Dark in the cab. I praised the Lord for that piece of luck. I was getting too cocky. Driving by the ranger station. But even with my mistakes, you wouldn't of caught me without Tony. Smart boy. He outsmarted me. Never thought he'd be crazy enough to jump into Elk Creek. He knew he had to get below the Choke, and he made it. I looked downstream as long as I dared. Figured he got caught in the undertow and was at the bottom of the hole. Where'd you find him?"

"More than a mile downstream. He crawled under some low hanging branches before he passed out."

"I looked that far. Smart boy. He okay now?"

"Recovering."

"Good. He had God on his side. Should of just run when he figured me out. Can't mess with God's people. Those others, God didn't care about. Rich snobs. Too busy for God and He was too busy for them. But when I tried to kill one of His own, He put a stop to me."

The tape ended and Tony switched the TV off. He said nothing for so long that Garret finally spoke.

"He cooperated to avoid the death penalty. But all through the interview, he kept saying that God wanted him to spill everything. I made a point of telling him which killings you'd tied to him. He was actually proud of you. We'd never seen anything like it."

"So I won't have to testify."

"No. He agreed to life without parole in exchange for his cooperation. He showed absolutely no remorse for any of the killings. In his mind, rich snobs deserve to die. Killing Phillips and Egan, he found sad, but necessary. He really regretted shooting you. He asked about you several times."

"You think he's sincere?"

"Yes. And so did the shrink who watched the interview."

"Did you figure out where he developed a pathological dislike for wealthy people?"

"Particularly those that fancied themselves outdoorsmen. Do you remember his first victim?"

"Hamilton?"

"Yeah. Killed in the Appalachians a dozen years ago. CEO of Hamilton & Sons Corporation, now known as HNS Corporation."

Garret drank his coffee until Tony made the connection.

"Gil's boss? He killed his boss?"

"From all accounts, the man was an SOB. But rather than quit, Simon hunted him down like an animal. Investigators had so many suspects, they didn't notice a lowly traveling salesman. Hamilton had just engineered a hostile takeover. He'd filed for divorce and his wife stood to lose everything. He'd fired his vice-president. Nobody really mourned his death."

"So Gil got away with killing his boss and decided to get rid of more wealthy people."

"He not only got away with it. In his mind, he was rewarded for it. Hamilton's estranged wife took over the company. Made dramatic changes. Simon got a promotion. All employees were treated better. He saw it as a sign that he'd done the right thing. Made the world a better place for the working man."

"He thought he had God's approval."

"Some kind of blue collar avenging angel."

"Hamilton was a rugged, macho type?"

"The great white hunter. Every picture I've seen of him had animal trophies in the background. That's why Simon killed him like he did. He believed that if any of them ever escaped, then God wanted them to live. Each success just left him more convinced that he was doing the right thing. You're the only one who got away."

"Did you ask him if one came close? Because he wounded them before he started his hunt."

"Yes. It happened early in his career. Back east. He didn't see wounding them as tipping the odds in his favor. After all, he never shot them in the leg the first time or even the second. They could still run."

"That was the difference with the copy cat."

"Right. A lot shorter blood trail."

"That's it then."

"Just tying up loose ends."

Tony sighed.

"What a summer."

"Not what you expected when you left the seminary last spring. Any regrets?"

"About leaving the seminary? No. I could have skipped being hunted and shot. But no. No regrets. I'm just where the Lord wants me to be."

"You're right where I want you too. I'd hate to try and pull you away from preaching a sermon to help me with a back country investigation."

Tony laughed.

"Give me more time to heal before you pull me anywhere."

###

About The Author

Paula F. (Pfeiffer) Winskye began writing novels about girls and horses at age 12. For more than 30 years, she continued to write for her own enjoyment. She credits her husband, John, with encouraging her to publish her novels.

She released the first, *James Collins: Royal Entanglements* in 2002. *James Collins: Cowboy Prince* followed in 2003; *Collins Family Reunion* in 2005; and the romance, *Greener Pastures* in 2006.

The Reverend Finds His Calling is Winskye's first mystery. She is currently working on another Tony Wagner mystery and planning the release of the next installment in the Collins Family Saga.

A native of New Rockford, North Dakota, Winskye and her husband raise Tennessee Walkers on a small farm near Sheyenne, N.D. She has one step-son, Joe.

Learn more at winskyebooks.us